Delana tried to stand but toppled from the unexpected burden of Dustin's boots on her pooled skirts.

"You're stepping on my dress!" As she lost her balance, his arm shot out and snaked around her waist.

"Gotcha." With her pressed to his side, Dustin wanted to taste her sweet lips in the afternoon sunshine. He contented himself with offering her a raspberry. "I'd say we deserve a little reward."

"Mmmm." She savored the luscious fruit before selecting another. "Here's one for you—if you've any room left in your stomach."

"I did put away a lot of that fried chicken," Dustin agreed before accepting the proffered fruit.

"Ah." Delana raised a brow. "I thought you might be full from all the raspberries you've sneaked."

Dustin stopped chewing and gaped at her. "You knew?"

"Of course I knew." She giggled. "I thought it was funny, how you'd look so pleased with yourself every time I turned back around."

"What gave me away?" He set down the pail.

"The juice on your chin." She reached up to brush it away with her fingertips.

Dustin held his breath at the softness of her touch. *Lord, this day of rest has made me anxious to finish my work. The second cabin must be built before the circuit preacher comes.* Delana put her hand on his forearm, bracing herself as she lifted their harvest.

And, Lord? Please let ~~_____~~ *soon!*

KELLY EILEEN HAKE

Hello! This is my fifth Heartsong Presents title with Barbour Publishing. I've also released three novellas in Barbour anthologies while earning my BA in English. Currently, I'm working toward earning my credential so I can teach high school English, but plan to continue writing. It's far too much fun to give up!

Books by Kelly Eileen Hake

HEARTSONG PRESENTS

A Time
to Plant

Kelly Eileen Hake

Heartsong Presents

To the Creator of all things, and for all with a spirit of adventure and a heart for the Lord.

A note from the Author:
I love to hear from my readers! You may correspond with me by writing:

Kelly Eileen Hake
Author Relations
PO Box 721
Uhrichsville, OH 44683

ISBN 978-1-59789-469-2

A TIME TO PLANT

Our mission is to publish and distribute inspirational products offering exceptional value and biblical encouragement to the masses.

PRINTED IN THE U.S.A.

prologue

March, 1864

My Dearest Dustin,

It is with a heart made heavy with grief that I write this letter. After months of prayer that Hans was still alive and simply missing, we've received word that he lost his life at Vicksburg. I will never see Independence Day in the same light again, as the freedom for others has been purchased, in part, with my brother's blood.

Nor does our sorrow end there, for Papa passed on to heaven a week past. I wonder whether he would have had the strength to conquer the cholera had he not been weakened in spirit by the loss of his eldest son.

Mama is so beside herself that she's not slept since Papa died. The doctor dosed her with laudanum that she might have healing rest. I mourn with her for Papa and Hans. So much loss in such a short span of time—I fear my own heart would break were it not for the grace of God and my dreams of our future as man and wife.

Father's final instructions were to sell the house and mercantile immediately, pack all we could need, and join you on the homestead as soon as possible. It is far sooner than we'd planned, I know, but I long for the solace of your smile. This year has passed so slowly without you.

Our party is much larger than anticipated. Mama and Isaac will come with me, as Jakob is now the head of our family. She will write to Jakob herself, so you men will be receiving her solemn letter as well as mine. Mama refuses to leave the Bannings behind, as they've become more than cook and stable master and seem like family. Cade and Gilda are joining us, along with their daughter, Kaitlin, who has a surprise for Arthur when we arrive. I'm sure he'll be glad to see his wife again after so long an absence.

Not to worry, though. I'll be bringing along absolutely everything we could possibly need. I'm making the arrangements for train and steamboat but wanted this letter to arrive as far ahead of us as possible. Pray that God grants us traveling mercies as we leave Baltimore to join you in the wilds of the frontier. Our party should arrive sometime in April, though I cannot be sure when. I come determined to work alongside you as helpmeet and make our spread a home.

With sincere affection,
Delana Albright

one

April, 1864

"We've done well," Dustin Friemont declared to his partners as they sat down for the midday meal. "At this rate, we'll finish right on time." He sat with his back against the barn, flanked by his future brother-in-law, Jakob Albright, and their friend, Arthur MacLean.

"My sister comes in just over a year." Jakob batted away a few gnats. "We're running out of time."

"Not really." Dustin Friemont lifted a gloved hand to shade his eyes from the glare of the bright sun as he surveyed his surroundings with satisfaction. Majestic mountains overlooked a forest of timber, which gradually gave way to the meadow alongside a fresh creek. He knew Delana would love the land he'd chosen for their home. "We've got a tight schedule to keep, but things are going better than I'd hoped."

"Eleven months of hard labor and we've precious little to show for it." Jakob bit into a piece of jerked beef and yanked some free.

"There's 480 acres among the three of us," Dustin mused, "and in eleven months we've filed our claims and begun the work of proving up."

"*Begun*," repeated Jakob pessimistically, "is the right word. We don't have so much as a house raised."

"Dinna be forgettin' my smithy." Arthur MacLean flexed his powerful muscles in a mighty stretch. "A lot of work went into that."

"And a lot of work comes out of it." Dustin slapped Arthur on the back. "Without your repairs to plow and sodbusters we would never have been able to clear as much as we have."

"We have to do better this year." Jakob slurped some water. "The first year we couldn't expect to cultivate nearly enough land, but now is the time to expand. We need to raise a house for Delana. My sister is not going to live in a barn."

"Of course not!" Dustin ripped a piece of jerky with his teeth.

"Nor my wee wife." Arthur frowned. "My Kaitlin is deservin' of a real home."

"And she'll get it." Dustin brushed dust off the seat of his britches. "So enough sitting in the shade. If we've all eaten our fill of dinner, we'll get back to clearing this field."

As he worked alongside his partners, Dustin's thoughts turned to God.

Every hour spent and every ache endured is well worth it. I've been away from my Delana for so long now, Lord. It's been months since I've had so much as a letter. Please let all be well with her. I thank You for the labor that occupies my hands and distracts my heart from the distance between us. With every step I take, I clear not only the land for crops, but also the way for a new life. Please give me continued strength so I can have all in readiness for my bride. We have much to accomplish, but I know we can succeed in You. Let me prove to Delana that I will be a good provider when she arrives, Lord.

Thirteen months. . .only thirteen more months. . .

&

"Only three more days." Delana answered Captain Massie's question as they oversaw the unloading of all her gear from his steamboat, the *Twilight*. "It will take three days of traveling southeast from Fort Benton to my fiancé's claim."

"And my son's," Mama added.

"I wish you the best." The gallant captain smiled at them both. "I've never seen a frontier bride with such a large entourage."

"We've come to build a life, Captain Massie." Delana surveyed the wagonloads of goods. "It will take more than this to succeed."

"It takes strong will and a stout heart," the captain agreed.

"And God's grace," Delana added. When she realized that she'd frowned at the captain for the omission, she softened her expression. "The help of gentlemen like yourself has also proven valuable."

"Indeed." Massie grinned, and Delana suspected he was thinking of the fees he'd earned for transporting so many passengers and such an outrageous amount of freight.

"Your expertise has eased our way," Delana praised. "If you hadn't advised us to purchase livestock in Kansas City, we'd have been in trouble when we found very little is available here at Fort Benton."

"Certainly not in the quantity you acquired." Massie watched as dockworkers unloaded one hog, three sows, four dairy cows, thirty-five baby chicks, and two mares. "I'll be leaving you fine ladies now to attend to other matters." With that, he headed down the gangplank.

"I'm glad to see they've unloaded the oxen for the freight

wagons." Mama finally tucked her wrung-out hanky into her reticule with a sigh of relief.

"Four teams of six oxen," Cade Banning confirmed. "One for each freight wagon."

"How's it going, Cade?" Delana knew he'd been below deck, supervising the transport of their precious livestock.

"Well, they know what they're doin'. I've hired four fellas who've agreed to load us up and drive the freight wagons to our spread in return for a team of mules, one of the buckboards, and provender for their journey to Virginia City. They're going to try their luck at finding gold in this territory." Cade shrugged. "I figure you will want to join Gilda and Kaitlin, to see with your own eyes where everything is."

"Where will you be?" Delana wondered aloud, anxious to keep her group together. Isaac had threatened to join the war several times since the news of Hans's death.

"Takin' young Isaac to market to purchase mules for the buckboards and see if'n we can't find a guide to the spread."

"Thank you, Cade, for keeping track of my brother in addition to overseeing that matter." Delana saw the dockworkers stacking all the cut lumber into one of the freight wagons. She rushed over. "No, no, no! If you put some of that in the bottom of each wagon, it will make the load more even." The men grumbled but parceled out the lumber among the four wagons.

"What do you want in this one?" A man jerked a grimy thumb toward the freight wagon behind him.

"These trunks." Delana pointed to the teetering pile. Each one held clothing or items of a personal nature. "And this." She lovingly ran her hand over the varnished oak of her hope chest.

Kaitlin walked by, carrying a crate full of bolts of fabric. This, too, went in the first wagon. Delana's traveling writing desk and the women's sewing boxes and medicine chests rounded out the first load. The final item to find its home inside was the crate of Papa's books Delana refused to leave behind. *Papa.*

"And this one?" A tall man forced her attention to the next wagon.

"That stove." Delana gestured to the first cast iron appliance. "The other needs to be in the third." The stoves were the heaviest items they'd brought with them—and arguably the most important.

Delana directed the men, watching as pots, pans, skillets, Dutch ovens, a clockwork jack, roasting pans, baking trays, mixing bowls, and everyday dishes slowly filled the second wagon.

Gilda oversaw the third load of freight, zealously guarding the dried meat, baking supplies, canned vegetables, jars of preserves, and an array of spices. The dry goods took up a fair amount of space.

Mama hovered around the last freight wagon, watching the workmen like a hawk. Great-Grandma's rocking chair, *Grossmutter*'s glass dishes, and Mama's china were carefully tucked inside. The wall clock from Papa's study, and the tintype photos of their relatives rested alongside galvanized tubs, rolled up rugs, and bedding.

Cade had already seen to the three buckboards. All farming implements, tools, feed for the livestock, and the water they'd need for the trip had already been secured. With the exception of the piglets and chicks, the rest of the livestock would walk for three days until reaching the barn her fiancé and brother had built.

The sun began to set, but Cade and Isaac had not yet returned. *Lord, please let them be all right.*

Delana tamped down the fear that her younger brother had run off. *What's left of our family must stay together.*

"Isaac and Cade!" Mama's relieved cry reassured Delana. Since Hans and Papa had died, Mama had been uneasy whenever Isaac or Delana were out of her sight.

"Who's that with them?" Delana squinted but could only see the shadow cast over the third man's face by his hat brim. He stood far taller than Cade, about the same height as Dustin and with the same confident stride. . .

Can it be? Did he get my letter and travel to Benton to wait for me? Has my fiancé come to take us home? She shifted and craned her neck, trying desperately to catch a glimpse of his face.

He lifted his head, and Delana tried to tamp down the swell of disappointment. This stranger was far older than her Dustin, with a full beard and wide grin.

"Hello." Delana pasted a welcoming smile on her lips after Cade introduced everyone to Rawhide Jones.

"Rawhide?" Mama's tone rang with scorn, her eyebrows raised disapprovingly.

"Right you are, *Bernadine*."

The man grinned as Mama spluttered in surprise and grew red in the face. Delana realized her mother did not like this man knowing more about her than she did him. Dustin must have talked about his bride-to-be and her family to Mr. Jones. The thought pleased her.

"Glad you decided to dispense with the formalities," Rawhide continued to Mama. "Highfalutin ways aren't practical on the plains. It's good to see you've the sense to recognize it."

Mama's mouth opened and closed like that of a landed fish, but she couldn't seem to find the words. Since she'd set the tone by using his Christian name first, a reprimand wouldn't do. Rawhide's irreverent attitude apparently irked Mama, even as his compliment obviously sealed his rejoinder with the stamp of courtesy. Delana bit back her own smile.

"Though I believe I'll still call you Miss Albright." Rawhide swept his well-worn hat off his head and lowered his voice. "Unmarried young females are scarce in these parts, and we don't want to encourage unwarranted familiarity by the men. With that in mind, you can call me Rawhide, but I'll be addressing you real proper."

"Thank you," Delana murmured.

"You're every bit as lovely as your fiancé said." Rawhide turned back to her mother. "And it's easy to see who lent you her beauty."

Mama glowered at him in stony silence.

"My fiancé?" Delana laid a gloved hand on his arm. "You know Dustin Friemont?"

"Yep." Rawhide rocked back on his heels. "I know everyone within five days' travel from here. That's why Mr. Banning"—he jerked a thumb toward Cade to punctuate the comment—"has asked me to guide you to the homestead."

"*Wunderbar!* It's wonderful!" Mama, obviously recalling her priorities, deigned to give the man a slight nod. "I'm sure we can rely upon your"—her magnanimity ostensibly deserted her as she searched for an appropriate word—"knowledge."

"I know the easiest routes and the best areas for hunting

along the way. Even so, this is a large group with a lot to haul." He cast an assessing glance at the newly packed freight wagons and buckboards. "It'll be a solid three-day journey if all goes well."

"Can you tell me how he and Jakob are?" Delana longed for any news of them.

"And Arthur?" Kaitlin chimed in, apparently just as eager for information about her own husband.

"They're doin' right well." Rawhide slapped his hat on his head. "For now, I suggest you turn in early. We leave at sunup."

❧

"I can't believe it." Dustin squinted at the horizon.

"Believe it," Jakob stated with grim satisfaction, rolling his shoulders to ease the ache.

"Our first forty acres." Dustin gulped huge mouthfuls of lukewarm water thirstily before continuing. "We have five years to cultivate this much on each of our homesteads, or we won't have proved up."

"At this rate," Arthur mused, "that will mean it'll be another three years afore we've done the minimum."

"Not so," Dustin refuted. "We've done much in addition to clearing forty acres. We'll need not raise barn nor smithy this year."

Arthur brightened and slapped Dustin on the shoulder. "So long as we work together, we'll come out far ahead of those who go it alone."

"This summer, while the wheat and corn grow, we'll need to be making things ready for our brides." Dustin conjured up the image of a cozy log cabin waiting for Delana. She'd arrive at a time such as this, with the big blue sky stretching over still-snowcapped mountains and green meadows made cheerful with wildflowers.

Lord, help me have all in readiness for her. Let her look on this land with the love and pride I do. The timing is good for her to see our homestead at its finest. Let me be a good steward of the land You've given us.

Dustin dipped his canteen in the stream in preparation for returning to work. When a flock of startled birds rose from the trees ahead, he turned and snatched his shotgun from his saddlebags.

"Bear?" Jakob grabbed his own shotgun, ready to shoot if need be.

"Could just be a coyote," Arthur reasoned. "Or a mountain lion."

"Whatever it is, it could be dangerous." A predator, a dry spell, forest fire, locusts, sickness—anything was a threat to their carefully laid plans. Dustin listened intently, recognizing the sound of many horses or head of cattle. "Claim jumpers." He kept his defensive stance. No group of ranchers or fellow settlers would take his land. Whoever was coming, they'd be leaving just as quickly.

"Easy!" Rawhide rode into the clearing, and the men swiftly lowered their guns.

"What's coming, Rawhide?" Dustin heard ominous creaks and shouts amid the heavy plodding of hooves.

"More trouble than you can possibly imagine."

two

"A freight wagon?" Dustin stared in disbelief as the thing came swaying into view.

"More than one." Rawhide stooped and took a draught from the cool stream.

"They can't pass through our land!" Dustin raised his voice to be heard.

"Oh, they won't be." The older man's exasperating answer was accompanied by a mischievous grin.

"*Who* won't. . . ?" Arthur's voice faded as his eyes widened in obvious recognition of the first figure stepping onto the meadow. *"Kaitlin?"* The blacksmith rubbed his eyes vigorously before confirming the sight of his young wife. "KATIE!" He gave a mighty whoop and broke into a run. In just a minute, he was gathering his prize in his arms and spinning 'round before kissing her soundly.

It's all right. Dustin quickly began to reconfigure their plans. *Kaitlin missed Arthur and came early. It's just one woman, and it looks like she brought plenty of supplies. We can adjust. . .* His reassurances fell flat when a second freight wagon followed the first.

All right. Rawhide must have brought a really large shipment of coal for Arthur's forge. Maybe he struck an unbelievable bargain, and it'll be worth the bother of unloading so much. After all. . . He caught sight of a second figure stepping into view.

"Mama?" Jakob's disbelieving voice wavered on the too-still air before he started toward his mother.

Mama Albright? Why would Kaitlin bring Mrs. Albright all the way out here? A sudden realization stabbed his heart. *Hans must have died. She has traveled all this way to tell Jakob and to fetch him back to Baltimore to be his father's heir.* He straightened his shoulders against the loss of a big part of their work force.

We'll still be fine. Mrs. Albright won't stay long, so she's not a major concern. The thing to remember is that Delana isn't here. I still have a year to build our home into something worthy of her. If she'd traveled with her mother, she'd have led the bunch. She's always running ahead, but she didn't now. That means we'll be okay...

The warm sensation of deep relief vanished as the wail of an infant rent the air.

No. His mind refused to believe the message relayed by his ears. He shook his head back and forth to stop hearing the impossible sound. That failing, he gave the side of his skull a good *thunk*, which did nothing but give him a bit of a headache.

Cade and Gilda Banning walked up to where Arthur still held their daughter tightly. Dustin watched as Gilda transferred a small, swaddled bundle to Arthur's arms. The look of awe and fear on the big blacksmith's face made Dustin groan.

He desperately sought for a bright spot in what was rapidly becoming a disastrous day. A smaller man joined Jakob and his mother. *Ahhh...she brought Isaac to guard his brother's claim. She should have sent him alone—at fifteen he's old enough, but there's no telling what goes on in the mind of a woman. The important thing is that Delana is back in Baltimore, minding the mercantile with her father. Thank You, Lord, for giving me time to prepare for her. A proper young lady like my love needs to come home to. . .well, a house. Thank You!*

His breath rushed out of his lungs in a whoosh as a slight figure with golden curls and blue skirts stepped into the meadow. Dustin's heart sank as his very worst fear headed straight for him. *Delana.*

❧

Dustin. If he only knew how thoughts of him had sustained her through the arduous journey.

Dustin, she'd thought as she packed for the trip while Mama cried at leaving their home. *Dustin,* she'd promised herself when the babe cried nonstop on the train. *Dustin,* she'd held to his memory while she fought her tumultuous stomach on the Missouri River. *Dustin,* she'd searched for any hint of him during their three-day trek from Fort Benton. And now, here he was, speechless with joy at the sight of her.

"Dustin!" She threw herself into his arms, nestling close to his chest and holding him tight. "Oh, Dustin. . ." The moment she'd been living for, for the past weeks, had finally come! "I'm so glad to see you." She laughed. "Even with that silly beard covering half your face."

"Delana." His deep voice, so low and private, rumbled through her.

"I'm here." Relief mixed with the joy, and tears slipped down her face as he drew back and tilted her chin upward.

"What are you doing here?" A strange gleam glinted in his brown eyes, and his mouth set in a harsh line.

"I. . .I came home," she stammered, wondering what could

possibly be wrong when they were together.

"Your home is in Baltimore." He seemed to realize the effect of his flat tone and softened it. "At least, it is for another year."

"You didn't get my letter!" She pushed away from him, finally understanding what troubled him. "You didn't know we were coming." Her voice sounded small and forlorn even to her own ears.

"No, I didn't." Dustin crossed his arms over his chest but didn't break eye contact. "What did it say?"

She reminded herself of all the things he didn't know in an effort to overlook the one thing her heart knew all too well: he was not pleased to see her.

"Hans fell at Vicksburg," she began shakily and then continued with more confidence as he stepped nearer and reached for her. "Papa died of cholera last month."

"Oh, Delana." He gathered her in his embrace, one hand cradling the crown of her head against his strong shoulder. "I'm so sorry."

"It's been so hard," she mumbled against the linen of his shirt. *But I don't have to be strong alone anymore. You'll stand by me and understand.*

"My poor, sweet Delana." He pressed his cheek to hers.

She pushed against his solid chest to look up against him. "Now that we're here, it will all be okay." Tears of joyous relief streamed down her face.

"How does being here make it okay?" His brow furrowed.

"Because we're together." She summoned a brave smile and reached up to cup his face. "We're all together, as a family should be."

"Honey," he took her hand away from his bearded jaw and held it in his work-roughened palm. "This isn't the place for you."

"Why not?" Delana searched his gaze. "What other place can be better than at my husband's side?"

"At your mother's, as we planned."

"But I am." She didn't understand. Surely he could see Mama right over there, with Jakob and Isaac.

"And it was good of her to travel with you." He moved to hold both her hands together before continuing, "But you'll need to go back with her for now."

"Go back?" She frowned before realizing that he didn't know Mama and Isaac and the Bannings would all be staying. "I'm so sorry you didn't get my letter, Dustin." She willed him to understand. "We're here for good. All of us."

"All of you? Where will you stay?"

Delana noticed the tightness in his jaw and hurried to reassure him.

"Cade and Gilda will claim their own land. They say they don't mind bunking in the barn until they have a place. Isaac and Mama will stay with Jakob, and of course Kaitlin and little Rosalind will live with Arthur." She nodded, encouraging him to see the practicality of the plan.

A strangled groan rumbled out of Dustin as he pulled a bandana from his back pocket and mopped his brow. He gazed at the four freight wagons, three buckboards, and everything else around him in disbelief.

"We've come prepared."

He made another one of those strangled-sounding groans, and she patted him on the arm. "I know it's a change in plans," she soothed. Allowances had to be made for his reaction. Dustin was nothing if not methodical, and she'd just waltzed into the middle of his careful plans. "I assumed you'd get my letter and know we were coming. Take all the time you need to let it sink in."

He gave a jerky nod. Silence stretched between them, and Delana waited patiently until she realized that he might take longer than she thought.

"Dear?" She patted his chest. "While you think it over and maybe talk to Rawhide about the cattlemen we hired to drive the oxen back, we ladies would appreciate a chance to wash up and such." When he didn't respond, she tried again. "Why don't you just tell me where the house is, so we can start getting settled in?"

Raucous laughter made her start with fright. She turned her head to see Rawhide laughing so hard he was doubled over.

"Oh, dear!" She rushed over. "Has the heat gotten to him?" she asked Dustin as their guide struggled to draw a breath.

"No." Dustin kicked at the grass. "It's not the heat."

"Maybe we should get him to the house and have him lie down a bit," Delana worried.

"The house!" Rawhide echoed and hollered with laughter anew, tears of mirth streaming from his closed eyes.

"Yes." Delana straightened up. "You carry him to the house while I fetch our medicinal supplies. It's good that we came in time, as it's obvious some malady has befallen him."

"It sure has!" Rawhide snickered. "Women!" he gestured toward her and Mama, who'd come to stand by her side.

"Don't pay him any attention." Dustin stepped on his friend's boot. "All that's wrong with him is a busted funny bone."

"I'm not so sure. . .He needs water and rest, at the very least," Mama declared. "Let's get him inside."

"Don't you get it?" Rawhide wiped his eyes, took a few deep breaths, and continued in spite of Dustin's beleaguered sigh.

As Delana's heart sank, Dustin met her gaze with a pained look.

"We haven't built a house yet."

three

Rawhide is laughing at me. Look at Delana—the shock and disappointment in her eyes. And Mama Albright is glaring fit to beat the sun. Everyone knows it's the man's job to provide for his family, and I've failed. She came to me, having lost the head of her household, and the house itself, looking to make a home with me. What can I offer her? Nothing. Lord, why is she here? Why could I not have received the letter so I'd have built some kind of house for her? What am I to do now?

First things first. Dustin upended his canteen over Rawhide's head, jolting his friend out of his inappropriate laughter.

"This can't be true." Delana's disbelieving whisper sent a sharp pain through Dustin's stomach.

"Yes, it's true." He squared his shoulders, praying they were strong enough for the burden now placed upon them. What he'd planned and dreamed would be a happy reunion had become a daunting reality instead.

"Oh." Delana seemed at a loss for words.

"What do you mean, 'it's true'?" Delana's mother demanded forcefully. "I cannot believe that after days on a sooty train, several more on a wavering steamboat, and three more jouncing on buckboards across the plains, we find ourselves *homeless!*" Her voice rose steadily throughout the indignant speech, ending on a note so shrill, Dustin fought not to wince.

"Mother!" Delana's shocked outrage surprised all of them.

"Dustin knew nothing of our impending arrival. He never received my letter!"

Now my bride is fighting my battles for me? But what could he do but give her the curt nod she was obviously waiting for.

"And I'm assuming that Jakob never got the one you wrote to him." She looked to her brother for confirmation.

"No." Jakob looked as chagrined as Dustin felt.

"Umm. . ." Mama Albright shifted her gaze to the bedraggled fringe of lace on her sleeve. "Well, you know how. . . distracted I was after your father's death. . ." Her words trailed off into an indistinct mumble.

"I only found out about Hans and Papa moments ago." Jakob's jaw clenched, and Delana hugged him before turning to her mother.

"You—you never wrote one?" Delana's quiet disbelief carried more weight than her anger moments before. She closed her eyes for a moment, drawing a deep breath. "The important thing is. . ."

"Is what, exactly?" Jakob's voice sounded oddly hollow in his fresh grief.

"Is that everyone arrived safely," Dustin announced. Delana's grateful smile spurred him on. "We're all hale of body, and now that we're together"—he clamped an arm around her waist as though to illustrate the point—"we're whole of heart, too."

In a silent but obvious show of her support, Delana snaked her arm around his middle and rested her head against his shoulder. The soft smell of lilacs drifted from her hair.

"Aye," Arthur agreed, "that we are." He cradled his babe in one arm and his wife with the other.

"We'll start building a house tomorrow." Dustin saw the

men around him nod in fervent agreement.

"And we womenfolk will start supper now." Gilda bustled up to them with her apron full of provisions. "Just give us a good cook fire, and we'll take care of the rest."

God bless Gilda. Dustin managed his first true grin since they'd arrived. "It's been far too long since any of us have had a decent meal."

"Hey!" The indignant chorus came from Jakob and Arthur.

"None of us has starved," Jakob protested.

"This from the man who undercooks biscuits," Arthur snorted.

"As if you don't burn everything you put your hand to." Jakob seemed to rally from the bad news, striving to gain some normalcy. "Comes from working the forge, I guess."

"Pah," Dustin scoffed. "As though anyone could tell the difference between your gruel and your gravy, Jakob."

"I've yet to drop the stewpot and spill our supper altogether," his soon-to-be brother-in-law grinned in silent recognition of Dustin's distraction.

"And not a one of you has started that cook fire." Kaitlin prodded her husband.

"Dustin?" Delana caught his attention once again. "You'll want to go with Rawhide and Cade. We've made arrangements with the freight drivers and cattle drovers already, but I'm sure you'll need to see to the details."

"Now that I can do." Dustin straightened his shoulders, gave Delana one last squeeze, and ambled over to the menfolk.

Immediately, Cade and Rawhide were eagerly explaining the agreements they'd made. "You'll have to decide how many head of oxen you want to keep for plowin' and such," Rawhide declared. "The cowboys will leave tomorrow to take the rest back to Fort Benton. Delana bought six of the beasts—any more than that will need to be purchased. The rest of the oxen were only rented."

"More than adequate," Dustin approved. *This way the oxen won't eat all the grazing or present any danger to the women.* "What about the drivers of the freight wagons?" He glanced uneasily at the small bunch of men seated by the creek.

"They'll be takin' one of the buckboards, a pair of mules, and provender for their journey to Virginia City." Cade gestured vaguely toward one of the wagons.

"That's more than generous." Dustin refused to belittle Delana's choices. *It's beyond generous—those drivers took her in. Not that there's much I can do about it now.* He chafed at finding yet another thing outside his control.

"Your fiancé struck a better bargain than that," Rawhide chortled. "She's got backbone, your little miss."

"She dealt with the hired men personally?" Dustin glowered at Cade. The man should know better than that after working for the Albrights the past decade and a half.

"No. The men gave me their askin' price," Cade replied calmly, "and I relayed it to her. She thought it over a bit and told me it was too dear. 'Cade,' she tells me, 'please go back and tell them we have a bargain only if they all agree to one month's worth of solid labor before they continue on their way.' "

"And they agreed to that?" Dustin marveled—the labor of four men for four weeks would do a lot for their farm.

"Not exactly. They countered with one week. That scrappy bride of yours settled in the end with two." Rawhide scratched his head. "Good thing, too. Miss Albright said somethin' 'bout how she reckoned they'd be useful for building another house for the Bannings. But now it looks like you'll be needing to tackle far more'n that."

"But their services will be greatly appreciated." Dustin quickly assessed their workforce. In addition to the three men already in residence, they now had Cade and Isaac, who was old enough to pitch in. The four drivers made nine men.

I've heard tell that two men can raise a log cabin in three days. 'Course, that's without the logs peeled and the notches made exact. Ours will be better than that. Still. . .in two weeks we should be able to build two homes and not fall too far behind with our plowing. Things aren't so bad after all.

ঙ

Things, Delana admitted to herself, were a lot worse than when they first arrived this afternoon.

Despite bone-weary fatigue and jostled muscles, the promise of reaching their new home before nightfall had proven an irresistible lure. They'd pushed hard to get here.

Now those aches returned with a vengeance, doubled by the harsh realities they'd discovered in the wilderness—no house, no warm welcome, not so much as a good cookstove.

Lord, I undertook this journey in the faith that this is where You meant me to be. That if I was obedient and of willing spirit, we'd arrive and Dustin would help make everything all right. I cannot pretend to understand Your ways—my sight is limited to the needs of my loved ones. You know us by name, unto the number of hairs on our heads, so You know, too, the pains of our hearts. What more am I to do, Savior? Please help me understand.

She blinked back the all-too-present tears. While she waited on the Lord, there was supper to be made for everyone. She hurried over to where Gilda presided over, not one, but two large cook fires.

The men had erected a makeshift crane from which to hang the massive stewpot and laid some of the planks Delana brought along over two large boulders in lieu of a table.

"Ah, Ana, love—" Gilda's smile raised Delana's spirits. "Would you help my Kaitlin with readyin' the vegetables?"

"Of course." She took an armload of carrots and onions over to the "table," where Kaitlin stood peeling potatoes. They worked in silence, the only sound the rhythmic *snick-thunk* of their knives slicing through the vegetables and onto the wood planks before them.

"Your mam is good with my babe," Kaitlin observed, looking to where Mama sat with little Rosalind cooing in her arms.

"She has soft hands and a loving heart," Delana agreed.

"A grandchild would go a ways toward fillin' the space left by your da and brother," Kaitlin ventured. "I wouldna mention it during the journey, but now that you're with Dustin, 'tis time to think on such matters."

"I. . ." Delana could feel the blush rising to her cheeks. *I can only pray that it will be so. A daughter to share her childhood with Rosalind, or a son with his daddy's grin. . .*Her hand involuntarily rested on her flat stomach, and a small smile flitted at the corners of her mouth.

"There, now, I didn't mean to embarrass ye." Kaitlin put down her knife. "But 'tis the way of things. Arthur and I were scarce wed a month afore he traipsed off with your intended and left me with Rosalind to warm my thoughts."

"They came to build a new life for us."

"Aye, and now they'll be buildin' new houses, too." Kaitlin grinned. "I heard the men speakin' 'bout how they'll sleep under the wagons until a home is raised. We women are to take o'er their quarters by the barn until then."

"Did you ever imagine that your babe would spend her first night on a new land in a barn?"

" 'Twas good enough for our Savior"—Kaitlin scooped the potatoes into her apron as she spoke—"so I'll not utter a word of complaint."

"What a wonderful way to see it." Delana filled her own apron with the carrots before walking over to Gilda's stewpot.

Gilda carefully added their bounty to the lard and beef broth simmering over the flames.

"Irish stew, is't, Mam?" Kaitlin sniffed appreciatively at the laundry cauldron Gilda had commandeered for the meal.

"Aye, 'tis. Now I'll be needin' you two to cut up one of those dried haunches of venison we purchased from Fort Benton. Ask Rawhide to fetch it for ye, along with our Dutch ovens."

"Would you like me to bring our Dutch oven, as well?" Delana offered as Kaitlin set off toward their guide. She looked at the three cowhands, four freight drivers, Rawhide, and their own group—quite a number of hungry men. Big as Gilda's stewpot might be, the men would eat far more.

"Kaitlin knows to bring all four, with so many men to feed who've not had a decent meal in months. We'll be makin' johnnycake instead o' biscuits this eve." Gilda carefully leaned over to add salt and pepper to the stew. " 'Tis simpler to mix and swifter to bake."

"I remember the ingredients from our lessons back home. I'll fetch them." Delana turned to go.

"Dinna forget the molasses and ginger," Gilda called after her. " 'Tis what lends the flavor!"

The three women worked feverishly for over an hour. Gilda watched the stew, adding marjoram and thyme, testing the taste, texture, and temperature time and time again. Delana and Kaitlin mixed huge batches of johnnycake batter while the Dutch ovens warmed amidst the ashes of the fires.

Delana threw herself into the task at hand, glad she'd been taking lessons from Gilda ever since learning she'd be a farmer's wife. *If there's one thing I can give Dustin, aside from responsibilities and worries, it's a good meal.* She slid pan after pan of the mixture into the useful contraptions, closing the ovens and heaping ashes on top to ensure even baking.

Soon she could feel tendrils of her hair sticking to her neck as she dashed back and forth. She knew her face would be flushed an unbecoming red, and her apron was smattered with flour. *Now's no time for vanity,* she chided herself. *Dustin will be focused on the food, not my face. A well-laden table will catch his eye far better than an immaculate dress. The smell of supper should give him more pleasure than any flowery perfume. A truly humble woman wouldn't even consider such things!*

But I am not truly humble, Delana realized, *for I wish more than anything that Dustin would look upon me and have cause to rejoice.*

four

Dustin pitched hay from extra stalls up to the loft at a frantic pace. Three dairy cows and two horses had just been added to the barn livestock.

"It was convenient, just grabbin' hay outta them stalls instead of goin' to the loft," Jakob muttered.

"Yeah, but that's what the loft's for. We just saved time the other way." Dustin worked the pitchfork vigorously. "We always planned on having more livestock."

"I know. But the dairy cows could wander."

"Then the women would have to hunt them down for the morning milking." Dustin rejected the idea. "Besides, it's still mighty cold at night."

"And we'll be sleeping under a freight wagon tonight." Jakob sighed.

"We'll all have to make concessions for a while. And remember," Dustin reminded, "the Lord loveth a cheerful giver."

"Cheery has never really been my way," Jakob pointed out.

"Then consider this a wonderful opportunity to grow spiritually." Dustin hid a grin when his friend refused to acknowledge that statement, and they worked in silence until the new animals were settled in.

With things well in hand, Dustin figured he ought to spruce up the room where the women would be sleeping. They'd bedded down in what would eventually be the tack room. He walked over to the doorway and stopped cold.

"What's wrong?" Jakob stood beside him and groaned. "It's a good thing there are only four women." He squinted at the small space.

"And a baby," Dustin tacked on. "How did it get so filthy?"

"This place isna fit for my bride." Arthur hulked in behind them.

Dustin eyed the motley assortment of hats, boots, lanterns, knives, and laundry. "Here's what we're gonna do. Jakob, grab those saddlebags hanging on the wall and stuff everything that's not garbage into 'em, according to who owns what. Be sure to throw away any refuse."

Jakob hopped to it, stuffing the bags with the evidence of a winter's worth of bachelor living.

"What about me?" Arthur shifted anxiously from foot to foot.

"Grab all the blankets you can find." Dustin sized up the blacksmith's beefy arms. "Take 'em outside and beat 'em within an inch of their lives. That'll remove some of the grit." As Arthur hustled past him into the room, Dustin grabbed his arm. "And Arthur? Be sure to do it behind the barn, out of sight of the ladies."

Dustin tromped over to the far corner of the barn, grabbing both rake and broom. They'd need to clear out the old straw they'd tracked in. He also grabbed a handful of nails and a hammer—the gals would need something to hang their garments from. *My bride may not have a proper house yet, but she'll have a roof over her head and a clean, warm place to sleep tonight.*

While the women cooked, the men worked steadily until they'd accomplished what seemed to him a major feat: The room looked habitable. Almost inviting even. Dustin grinned as he, Jakob, and Arthur clapped each other on the back.

"I'll bet it even smells better," Jakob stated before drawing a deep breath. His eyes closed in bliss and he sniffed deeply several times.

"It's nothing special." Dustin gave the man a puzzled look.

"No, it isn't." Arthur breathed gustily. "While we've been workin', the ladies hae been cookin'."

Dustin filled his lungs with air and his nose with the long-forgotten aromas of a well-prepared, hearty meal. "Smells good," he agreed.

The sound of a ladle banging loudly on a pot jerked them into action. *Suppertime!* Dustin scrambled to be the first through the doorway, racing the others out of the barn toward the delectable scents.

The slapdash "table" bowed slightly beneath the weight of a monstrous cauldron, which emitted the intoxicating aromas of meat and seasoning. Beside it sat pan after pan of what looked like cornbread, along with blackberry preserves and butter.

Cade blessed the meal, and they got down to business.

Gilda Banning stood at the head of the table, wielding her ladle like a general with his saber. Dustin fell into line along with the others, accepting a bowl and spoon from Kaitlin with a grateful smile. He proceeded to where Delana stood. For a second, he forgot about the food, just watching her as she sliced pieces of—

"Johnnycake?" She offered him a hefty wedge.

"Smells like heaven," Dustin praised as she smeared butter on the golden bread and passed it to him. He smiled his thanks and stood transfixed by the sudden brightness in her aqua eyes as she beamed back at him. "I'd forgotten how beautiful you are," he whispered.

"Oh, Dustin." Her rosy cheeks let him know she was flattered.

"Move along, Romeo." Rawhide nudged him in the ribs. "You're holding up the line."

"Yeah!" Jakob agreed from behind him. "That's practically a hanging offense tonight!"

"You're no Stuart Granville and his Vigilance Committee," Dustin shot back as he grudgingly moved along.

Rawhide refused to let him have the last word. "And you're no Henry Plummer!"

"If I'm not like Henry Plummer," Dustin considered as he came round the table to stand alongside Delana again, "then that means I *won't* be hung." Chuckles greeted his well-made point.

"Who's Henry Plummer?" Delana asked as she served more johnnycake.

"He was a sheriff in the territory who secretly created a band of outlaws to rob miners over by Virginia City." Dustin bit into his johnnycake and lost his train of thought for a moment.

"Isn't that just a ways west of here?" Delana turned to him, eyes wide with worry as her own supper remained untouched before her.

"A good ways," he reassured her after swallowing his first mouthful. "In January, Stuart Granville rustled up a Vigilance Committee to catch the thieves. When they found 'em, over two dozen men hung for their crimes, among them Henry Plummer."

"That's horrible!" Her hand covered her mouth. "No trial?"

"Not a court for days in these parts." Dustin shrugged. "Justice was served that night."

"What awful supper conversation." Delana hugged herself and frowned. "It's not humorous or entertaining in the least. It recalls tragedy and death and evil."

"You're right." Dustin put down his bowl of stew to rub her upper arms. As far as he was concerned, the fact that he'd abandoned such good food to comfort her spoke for itself. "Forgive me, sweetheart. We've been living as rough bachelors for far too long. A gracious meal deserves decent conversation."

She relaxed and nodded. He saw to it that she got her own helping of the food and walked her over to a large, flat stone, where they sat together near Arthur and Kaitlin.

"I'm sorry," Delana murmured as she picked at her food.

"For what?"

"For coming here without your knowing. I should have waited for you to write back." Her voice quivered and she curled forward.

"It's not your fault." Dustin scraped the bottom of his bowl. "If you'd waited, you would have had difficulties with the mercantile, and it could have been weeks before you got my reply. Think of it," he said bracingly. "I never got that first letter. You wouldn't have written another for a month. Then my response would've taken weeks before you could start the arrangements, and traveling in the heat of late summer is hard on the animals and tiring for the travelers. You did the right thing." He shifted so she couldn't see his face as he added, "Even though I wish it could have been different."

❧

Delana stiffened at his words. *I wish it could have been different.* The sentence echoed over and over in her mind, striking blows with as much force as a hammer.

He's still unhappy that I'm here. I thought he was softening, coming around to the reality of this. Lord, my heart melted when he smiled at me over by the table. And when he led me here, so we could sit together in the simple joy of one another's company, I felt more secure than I have in two months. Give me strength to prove it's right that I came. Let my hands be useful and my heart be open.

"I wish things could have been different, too," she said quietly.

I wish Hans were alive. I wish Papa had never gotten sick. I wish Mama had written to Jakob so at least one of the letters would have reached you. But most of all, I wish you would take my hands in yours and tell me you love me and can't wait until we're man and wife.

But she didn't say a word of all that. It did no good to complain, and she wouldn't have him pitying her. She wanted his admiration and acceptance, so she would make herself busy. Delana gently took his bowl and went to the stream to rinse their dishes before helping Gilda and Kaitlin clean the supper mess.

The days weren't at their full length yet, and darkness had enveloped the land by the time they finished. Arthur came up to Kaitlin after she'd nursed Rosalind beneath the privacy of a shawl.

"Let me take ye to your room for the night." He placed a huge hand on the small of her back and led her toward the barn. Not seeing Dustin anywhere, Delana hurried behind them.

Arthur led them inside the barn. A small room with four piles of fresh hay, covered with blankets, glowed cheerily by the light of a single lantern on an upturned crate. Another such crate supported a washbasin and pitcher.

"It's perfect." Kaitlin cuddled close to her husband.

"It's far from perfect," Mama disagreed as she entered the room. "Still, it's dry, enclosed, and will do for a short while."

Delana turned to see Dustin and Jakob's dark expressions as they stood across the barn. "Mama, you're tired. In the morning you'll see what a comfortable, warm place this is."

"We are blessed," Gilda declared as she stepped into the room. With that, everyone exchanged their good nights, and the men left.

"*Ja.* It's better than sleeping beneath the wagons," Mama conceded as she tested the give of the soft hay beneath their blankets.

"That 'tis," Gilda agreed. "Not that it'd make much of a difference to me tonight. I'll be asleep the moment I lie down."

"I think we all will." Kaitlin displayed baby Rosalind sleeping contentedly in her arms.

"Then we'd best say our prayers before we hit the hay." Delana had to smile as she finally understood the phrase.

The women stood close as Gilda began. "Dear Lord, thank You for giving us good weather and good men to help us on our journey. We're all here and healthy, and we've You to thank for it. Bless this night's sleep that we may arise in the morning ready to accomplish the work You've laid before us."

And help me to win Dustin's heart again, Delana added silently before raising her voice to join in, "Amen."

❧

"We're going to need more hay." Dustin surveyed the full barn.

"When will we scythe more grass if we still need to plow the clearing and build a cabin?" Arthur stopped mucking long enough to mop his brow.

"We'll find a way," Jakob promised, working faster. "At least we'll have good food and not have to waste time trying to cook it ourselves."

"That's true." Arthur brightened and grabbed his pitchfork once again. "I wonder what they'll make for breakfast?"

"It has to be better than cold biscuits," Dustin said thankfully. "And I want to tell you two that the cowboys are leaving this morning, but the freight drivers have pledged two weeks' labor."

"And I'm thinkin' 'bout staying on for a spell." Rawhide's voice came from the doorway.

"Oh?" Dustin raised his eyebrows in mute question.

"You could use an extra pair of capable hands," the older man pointed out.

"What's in it for you?" Jakob seemed suspicious.

"You mean aside from the fact I've eaten better the past three days than I have in the past three years?" Rawhide chuckled. "I aim to stick around to see you unload them wagons."

"Hey"—Arthur straightened up—"what is in all those wagons anyway?"

"I think," Dustin muttered, moving one last pitchforkful of

hay into place, "the question is more along the lines of what *isn't* in all those wagons."

"Seems like your bride packed half the world," Arthur mused. "I wonder if she brought anything useful."

"She has," Rawhide smiled mysteriously. "But for now, I think there are some matters you boys need to see to right away."

"Like what?" Dustin furrowed his brow. "We'll start hewing timber after breakfast."

"Good, but you all are missin' a few things aside from a house." Rawhide raised his brows.

"We haven't installed the water pump," Jakob groaned.

"Gentlemen," Dustin said grimly, "we've got bigger problems than a nonexistent water pump."

"Like what?" Jakob's exasperated tone said it all.

Dustin groaned. "I can't believe it didn't occur to me before."

"What?" Jakob fidgeted. "What else is on our plate?"

"Bad phrase, kid." Rawhide grinned.

"Men," Dustin squared his shoulders as he spoke, "what one simple thing can we do without, but ladies require?"

"A stove?" Arthur ventured. "We can order one of those."

"They've brought that," Rawhide volunteered.

"A washtub!" Jakob shouted, pleased with finding the answer.

"Brought that, too." Rawhide leaned against a wall, watching them expectantly.

"What is it, then?" Jakob glowered at Dustin, who rubbed the back of his neck.

"We never built"—Dustin took a pained breath before finishing—"an outhouse."

five

Delana heard a collective groan rise from the barn as she walked by. She poked her head through the doorway to see what was going on. "What's wrong?"

"Nothin'," Jakob hastened to answer. "Dustin just said something that he thought was funny, but it wasn't."

"You never were good at that." Delana smiled at her fiancé. "But what was the joke?"

"It wasn't really even a joke," Dustin admitted.

"All right, then." Delana backed up a step. "I came to tell you that breakfast will be ready just as soon as you wash up."

"That's the best news I've heard all day," Arthur told her.

"Well, it's not quite time, yet." Delana lowered her voice before explaining, "I thought you might need some extra time to shave your whiskers this morning."

"What's wrong with my beard?" Rawhide glowered at her.

"It's a very handsome beard," she soothed. "It's really more for Dustin and Jakob. See, last night Ma—" She belatedly broke off.

"Mama mentioned how bedraggled we all look?" Jakob filled in the blanks. "It was too much to hope she hadn't noticed."

"We hardly recognized the two of you when we arrived yesterday. Even after a year apart, I should know your faces in an instant."

"Mama's a stickler for those types of things," Jakob agreed.

"We'll take care of it."

"Thank you!" Delana turned to leave the barn. "Something familiar will make Mama feel more comfortable."

Dustin rubbed his jaw thoughtfully. "We'll see about hunting down a razor."

Delana watched, dumbfounded, as her brother grabbed a full saddlebag from the corner of the barn and began to rummage through it. Still more curious to her, Dustin joined him in pawing through the sacks.

"Actually," she called to them, "I did think to pack a few things."

"Like what?" Dustin turned around expectantly.

"Razors, strops, combs, shirts. . ." Delana gestured vaguely. "That sort of thing."

"Can you get to them easily?" Jakob couldn't hide his interest.

"Absolutely. Just give me a moment. . ." Delana turned to leave the barn but stopped for a moment. "It might be a good idea for you to gather up all your laundry." She cast a disparaging glance at the haphazard pile of saddlebags. "If Gilda's not using the cauldron for cooking today, we could do with a washday."

She left them dumping out the contents of bag after bag, pleased she'd found something that would prove useful to the men. When she reached the buckboard where the needed supplies were held, she had Isaac take everything back to the barn.

"Gilda," she called, moving toward the temporary outdoor kitchen, "will you be using the large cauldron today after breakfast?"

"With the cowboys leavin', I suppose I could make do with my largest pot," Gilda decided. "What did you have in mind?"

"Laundry."

"Hard work, but a good idea. We'll get the men into some of the new shirts we brought and wash all their clothes. It'll keep us busy while they start work on the cabin."

"Exactly." Delana looked at her own grimy dress. "And we've some things that could use a good scrubbing ourselves."

"Aye." Gilda nodded. "Since we won't be unpacking or settling in, all we have for the day is cookin'—and a simple fire doesn't lend itself to anything too fancy."

"What're you talking about?" Kaitlin came up, toting Rosalind. "This hasty pudding looks good to me!"

"We were thinkin' on makin' this a washin' day." Gilda wiped her hands on her apron. "After the cabin's up, we'll have a lot more to keep us busy."

"True enough." Kaitlin shifted the baby to her other shoulder. "I'm desperate to do Rosalind's nappies. She's a sweet one but messy for such a wee thing!"

"No messier than a group of bachelors." Delana groaned as she caught sight of the men approaching. Jakob, Arthur, Isaac, and Dustin each carried an armful of soiled linen.

"What's so funny?" Isaac looked at Gilda and Kaitlin, who were trying to suppress their mirth.

"Women talk." Delana grinned. "Why don't you men put up a good long clothesline while we get breakfast on the table?"

"Wait. . ." Gilda looked at the heap of laundry they'd left under a tree. "A small mountain of clothes, and that's only theirs! You men best string a few good long clotheslines if we're to hang all this!"

Mama oversaw the men while Gilda had Kaitlin and Delana laying out the butter, preserves, brown sugar, and fresh milk that would accompany the hasty pudding. Soon enough, thanks had been given and breakfast began. Everyone had a bowl of the hearty cornmeal mixture and doctored it with a choice of sweeteners.

"I always did like hasty pudding better than grits." Delana sat by Dustin.

"Mmmmhmmm." His response was muffled by a mouthful of mush.

"You clean up nicely." She stroked a finger along his freshly shaved jawline and smiled as he swallowed audibly. "I've missed you," she whispered.

"I missed you, too." He mumbled the words to his bowl, as though speaking to the food.

"But if you had your way, you would've gone on missing me." She set aside her breakfast, not hungry anymore.

"Yes." His jaw clenched as he spoke. "I didn't want you here like this."

"Neither did I." Delana closed her eyes. *I wanted to have the man I love greet me with affection and excitement, like Arthur did Kaitlin.*

"We'll just have to make the best of it." He rose abruptly and pushed his own empty bowl into her hands.

There was nothing left to say as she watched him walk away.

≈

The tasty breakfast he'd just eaten churned in Dustin's stomach. For a moment, he'd thought Delana understood that he'd wanted so much more for her.

I didn't want you here this way. He'd come as close as he

could to admitting how he'd failed her.

Neither did I. Her response showed him how wrong he'd been. Instead of telling him she was happy to be here, that she loved the land and was content to wait for the modern trimmings, she revealed her disappointment in him. She'd expected better and couldn't hide her feelings.

The only thing he could do about it was to start working—immediately. As he built their home, he'd restore her trust in him.

He saw the cowboys off with the bulk of the oxen before assembling the remaining men. The four freight hands, Cade, and Isaac had swelled their ranks, but—"Where's Rawhide?" He barely got the question out before shouts assailed his ears.

"How dare you?" Mrs. Albright was shrieking at poor, hapless Rawhide. "I am a"—her voice rose with each syllable until she shrieked the last word—"LADY!"

"Stop squawkin', woman!" Rawhide roared as he scrambled about, collecting the bits of laundry Dustin assumed Mrs. Albright had thrown at him.

"Squawking!" She spluttered before composing herself with a deep breath. "Listen to me, you unkempt brute—"

"Mama!" Delana had rushed over at the start of all the ruckus. Dustin met her there. "What on earth merits such upset?"

"That man handed me his"—Mrs. Albright raised a trembling finger toward Rawhide, delivering the last word in an appalled whisper—*"unmentionables!"*

"Here, now," Rawhide yanked on his askew hat as he broke in. "I was just givin' her my laundry. Gilda said it was washday."

"There, you see, Mama?" Delana patted her mother's shoulder. "He was just trying to keep everything orderly."

"Hmf." Mrs. Albright still glowered at Rawhide. "Since when does a man thrust his laundry into the arms of a grieving widow?"

"So you're not helping with the wash?" Rawhide cast an astonished glance from the small mountain of laundry beside them back to Mrs. Albright.

"Don't you even think of implying that I would shirk my responsibilities!"

"Make up your mind, woman!" Rawhide, having collected his scattered belongings, spoke loudly without actually bellowing. "Either you decide not to help"—he raised his eyebrows in a mute challenge and held out the clothes—"or you help your fine daughter and your friends with the laundry."

"Of course I'm helping." Mrs. Albright snatched the clothes from his outstretched arms as she all but spat out the words, "But you, sir, need to learn some manners!"

"True enough," the wily guide admitted. "I reckon you'll be helpin' with that, too." Not waiting for an answer, he turned to Dustin and rubbed his hands together. "Now, what have you decided to start with?"

"We'll be building the cabin on the cleared space nearest the barn," Dustin decided aloud. "It'll save us some time and will give the women space to plant a vegetable garden."

"And an orchard," one of the freight drivers added.

"What?" Jakob shot a quizzical glance at the speaker.

"The young miss brought saplings with her." Another man jerked a thumb toward the nearest freight wagon. "Apple trees, I was told."

"All right." Dustin took a moment to assess this new information. It would take the trees years before they yielded fruit, but planting them this spring would make it happen that much sooner. A source of fresh fruit could prove invaluable, and she'd even thought to bring his favorite.

"We need a man to dig an outhouse." Jakob gestured to the proposed site. "It has to be done today."

"I can do that!" Isaac volunteered. When some of the freight drivers chuckled at his enthusiasm, he reddened. "Better to build it now than clean it later."

"If it's all the same to you," Cade offered, "I'd like to see to putting up a water pump. It makes things easier for my Gilda when she's cooking."

"That'll have to wait until we order—" Dustin stopped when he saw the trusted friend shake his head. "Unless you thought to bring one?"

"Miss Albright thoughtfully packed one for each of us," Cade beamed as he spoke. "We have three."

"Sounds good." *One for the Bannings, one for the MacLeans, and one for Jakob's spread.* Dustin's swift tally demonstrated all too clearly that Delana had assumed he'd already have installed one for their home. He gritted his teeth and plunged ahead.

"So the rest of us need to get started chopping trees for logs and lumber." Dustin glanced at Cade. "If we don't have axes for each man, we'll work in pairs."

"We've three axes in addition to your four," Cade informed them, "and two, two-man saws."

"Excellent." Dustin looked at the four freight drivers. "Since you know each other, I'd ask you to divide into two pairs and use the saws. The rest of us will make do with axes until dinnertime. We'll be working to the west of the meadow.

Make sure you spread out so no one will be in the path of falling trees. Don't take ones that are too small to be of use, nor so large they would be a waste."

With that, the men filled their canteens, unloaded their tools, and bowed their heads for the day's blessing on their labor. "Lord," Dustin began, "we thank You for granting us friends to work beside and sharp tools to work with. We ask that You grant us the wisdom to use them wisely and safely." Before chorusing, "Amen," Dustin added a silent request. *And I ask, too, that we accomplish as much as possible so the women no longer have to bunk in the barn.*

six

"It's a good thing we brought more than one washboard." Delana straightened up and pushed a damp curl from her forehead. "Seems like there's not a single thing from the men that doesn't need a lot of elbow grease."

"Arthur's will always be that way—smithing is such dirty work." Kaitlin scrubbed a pair of her husband's sooty breeches with vigor. "The fact that none of those men probably thought to do laundry properly the entire time they were out here complicates things."

"You should see some of the stains on this old goat's shirts." Mama worked out her ire on Rawhide's laundry. "The man can't claim to be even halfway civilized!"

"He's no old goat," Gilda laughed. "I reckon he's close as can be to my age—and yours. Hard livin' makes a man rough."

"Why he chooses to scout and guide and hunt and trap in this wilderness, with no home to call his own, is beyond my understanding." Mama rinsed the hapless shirt and surveyed her work with obvious satisfaction.

"Dustin's letters mentioned something about him being a widower." Delana frowned and tried to remember how long it had been since Rawhide's wife passed on. It was no use. She'd have to wait until she could reach her writing desk, where she kept every letter her fiancé had written her.

"Oh!" Mama gasped and stopped what she was doing. "It's

a hard thing to lose your spouse." Her murmur carried all the pain of her own recent loss.

Mama didn't say anything else, but Delana noticed that she took more care with Rawhide's next shirt. *Shared sorrow deepens understanding and eases the way,* she realized. *If such a small bit of knowledge softens Mama's thoughts toward Rawhide, how close will Dustin and I become after building a home together? Lord, his words this morning hurt, but I still hope that we can settle into a good marriage.*

". . .weddin'." Gilda's voice captured Delana's attention.

"What did you say?"

"Head in the clouds already?" Gilda shook her head. "And here I was sayin' how at least your groom will have clean clothes for the weddin'."

"We don't know when that will be." Delana picked up another item to scrub.

"As soon as possible." Mama punctuated the declaration by snapping a pair of Rawhide's britches until dust swirled in the air.

"Arthur told me that we don't have a proper parson." Kaitlin sipped some of their fresh water. "The wedding will have to wait on the circuit preacher."

"Do we have any idea when he'll be here next?" Delana hoped her voice didn't betray her anxiety. *How long do Dustin and I have to rekindle our love before we're joined together as man and wife? How can I marry a man who is displeased with my very presence at his side? Lord, we need time to become re-accustomed to one another. I know we're a good match, but I worry that another such change in plans will leave Dustin unsettled.*

"There, there." Gilda reached over to pat her hand. "I'm

sure the lads will have your house built afore the time comes. You need not fear for your privacy."

Delana ducked her head to hide the hot blush she felt flooding her cheeks. To distract from her embarrassment, she gathered the scrubbed shirts and headed for the boiling cauldron. The heat from the fire and strong scent of lye gave a new reason for her flushed cheeks. She stirred the load with the long paddle they'd brought for that purpose, agitating the clothes so they'd wash thoroughly.

The hot work kept her hands busy while giving her time to clear her thoughts. When she returned to rinse the washed clothing downstream, she found Kaitlin nursing Rosalind.

"Here, let me help." Mama took the other side of the bucket containing the clothes from her arms. Together, they rinsed away all traces of the harsh lye before wringing them as dry as possible.

"Have we taken the clothespins from the wagons?" Delana turned to Gilda.

"They're in the bucket o'er by the wash line."

The cool, earliest hours of the morning passed by quickly, and soon it was time to start dinner.

"We'll be bakin' biscuits in the Dutch ovens." Gilda set about arranging the devices. "Thick slices of ham in the middle of the biscuits will make a hearty dinner."

"Ham sandwiches do sound good," Delana agreed.

"Crisp ham on hot, buttered bread will be simple to make in large quantity. Fresh milk alongside will finish the meal."

"How many batches will we need?" Mama looked at the Dutch ovens, then out toward the forest, where the sounds of chopping kept up.

"We'd best make plenty, so we'll have more for supper." Gilda laid out bowls and ingredients on their outdoor table. "Still more if we want biscuits and gravy later."

They mixed double batches, filling four pans for each round.

Hours later, they had a dozen batches of biscuits cooling on the table, with still more baking.

"If we do one more batch," Delana calculated, "we should have enough to last three days. Maybe we'll have a summer oven so we can bake bread after that."

"Aye." Kaitlin bounced Rosalind, who fussed a bit.

"Kaitlin," Delana called, "why don't you put her in her wicker basket for a nap?"

" 'Tis a good idea. I'll let her sleep while I slice the ham. That way, I'll keep her nearby."

The next hour flew by as they finished baking the bread. When Kaitlin stacked a heaping platter with cut ham, it was time to split the biscuits and make the sandwiches.

"Come and get it!" Delana called, ringing the dinner bell she'd unearthed from one of the buckboards.

Despite the distance to the forest and the noise from hewing logs, the men came running to wash up in the stream before receiving their food.

Delana walked about with a pitcher of milk kept cool in the stream. She poured it into tin cups as she greeted each of the workers after seeing to her fiancé first. When she reached Dustin again, he swallowed the last bite of his second sandwich, gulped down another cup of milk, and thrust the tin at her.

"Thanks," he said over his shoulder as he headed back to

the forest and away from her side for the second time that day.

❧

No matter how delicious the food tasted, Dustin forced himself to bolt it down and dash back to work. Daylight was too precious to waste a single moment. By staying on task himself, he set an example to the freight drivers as to what he expected.

The more logs they cut today, the sooner they could raise a cabin. Dustin swung his axe time and time again before he heard the sounds of sawing in the distance.

"Tim—ber!" He yelled before striking the last blows. With a mighty crash, yet another tree fell to the ground.

Breathing hard, he took off his hat and swiped at his forehead with a bandana. He gulped from his canteen, refreshing his parched throat as he looked over his handiwork. After the few moments he could afford to spare, he set about removing the largest limbs from the tree.

Dustin listened to every resounding crash with satisfaction as their team worked steadily through the hot hours of the afternoon. Time and again he hitched a fallen trunk to a team of oxen, driving them toward the building site. As the sun began to set, he pushed himself even harder. When Rawhide passed nearby, taking another log to the growing pile, Dustin spoke quickly, "Light's almost gone." He gestured toward the fallen tree he was stripping. "I figure the others will finish the work they're doing and call it a day."

"Most likely." Rawhide rubbed the back of his neck. "I reckon I can get this one to the clearing and fell one more, but I won't have light to strip the limbs."

"Sounds good." Dustin got back to work, determined to

finish hacking off the branches and to place this log on the pile. *Maybe if the pile of logs is large enough, it will show Delana and Mrs. Albright how seriously we're taking our work and how quickly we'll finish.*

He met his goal as dusk fell and ambled wearily to the stream. As he splashed cool water on his face and hands, washing away the dirt and weariness of the day, Isaac crouched down beside him.

"I dug the hole." Isaac plucked at some grass alongside the stream. "Built a raised seat, too."

"Good." Dustin nodded approvingly until the second part of his future brother-in-law's comment sank in. "What did you build a seat out of?"

"Some of the lumber we brought." The young man shrugged. "It didn't take hardly anything."

"How much lumber did you bring?" Dustin's mind spun with the possibilities.

"A freight wagon full."

"A team of only six oxen couldn't pull a freight wagon loaded with lumber." Dustin frowned at the incongruence.

"That's what the freight drivers told Delana, so she told them to put a fourth in the bottom of each wagon." Isaac stood up. "We put lighter stuff on top so the weight was even."

Floorboards. A loft. The outhouse. Doors and shelves. It's all more than provided for. For the first time in two days, Dustin felt lighter.

"Isaac, just what did you all bring?"

"Everything," Isaac said simply.

"I know about the"—Dustin paused before ticking off the items—"lumber, livestock, and tools. You obviously brought some food and clothing. . . what else?"

"Some food and clothing?" Isaac snickered. "The girls packed more food, blankets, linens, bolts of fabric, and clothes than you could believe."

"How—" The question died a short death as Dustin recalled the freight wagons. "What else?"

"Shotguns, canteens, rope—like I said, everything." Isaac shrugged. "What more is there?"

"I'm not sure." Dustin squinted in the sparse light. "Is there anything else for the house?"

"Rugs, some furniture, and, oh yeah, windows." Isaac sounded pleased with himself for remembering.

"Windows?" Dustin echoed in amazement.

"Nine-by-nine-inch panes, wrapped more carefully than a baby." He stopped talking when he heard the supper bell. "Food!"

Dustin understood that the rest of the conversation would have to wait. As they made for the campfire, his stomach growled.

"What's for supper?" Jakob sniffed hopefully at the bubbling pot.

"Welsh rabbit," Delana answered. She presented each of them with a tin plate filled with a large halved biscuit.

"Doesn't look or smell like any rabbit I've ever seen." Rawhide seemed puzzled.

"That's because it doesn't have a thing to do with rabbit." Gilda ladled a steaming stream into his dish. "It's melted cheese and butter with spices."

"I've never understood why they call it Welsh rabbit at all." Delana handed a plate to one of the freight drivers. "But I did add some dried powdered beef for flavor and succor."

"Hot!" Isaac yelped as he took an overeager bite.

"Good," Dustin praised around his own mouthful. Several of the men grunted their agreement. *It is good, but tomorrow I'll rise early and set some snares so the girls have fresh meat. I'll do everything I can to make this easier on them.* He savored the last bite on his plate before heading over for seconds. *And if they can make something this great out of bread and cheese, what can they cook up with a few real rabbits?*

seven

"Rabbits?" Delana looked askance at the brace of hares Dustin held out.

"I realized last night that we didn't have any fresh meat, so this morning I set some snares. I checked them when I knew it was about dinnertime." He looked at his catch happily. "They should make a fine supper tonight."

"Yes." Delana accepted the ties and forced a smile. *I thought he liked our cooking—he asked for seconds of the Welsh rabbit. But I suppose it just meant he was still hungry.* With a sharp pang, she suddenly knew the truth. *He believes I'm doing a poor job, so he's made sure tonight's supper will be satisfactory.*

She straightened her shoulders as she carried the six rabbits over to the area where they kept their kitchen supplies. *The corn chowder and biscuits should see him through until supper. I'll pull out all the stops tonight and show him what I can do.*

"Dustin snared our supper," she announced brightly, displaying the catch before setting it down. *A good wife supports her husband and praises him when he provides. That still holds true whether he hurt my feelings or not.*

She helped serve the hungry men before taking her own share. The sweet scent of the corn blended with the mouthwatering aroma of the bacon she herself had fried and chopped. Taking a biscuit from the depleted stock on the table, she looked around for Dustin.

I hardly saw him at all yesterday. Maybe if I sit beside him and tell him what I plan to make for supper, I can coax a smile out him before he rushes back to work.

But she couldn't find him among the others. She turned just in time to see him reach the pile of logs in the clearing. *He's avoiding me. This can't go on if we're to be man and wife.* Strengthening her resolve, she began to make her way toward him.

"*Nein, liebling.*" Mama's soft pressure on Delana's elbow stopped her.

"He's to be my husband." *And I love him.*

"And he will, but for now he's taking some time to work everything out." Her mother's smile softened the words. "Remember that it's the man who pursues his bride, not the woman who chases the groom."

"Aye," Gilda broke in as she walked up. "I ken what you're thinkin', lass, but you followed him all the way from Baltimore. When he's ready, he'll seek your company and the love you hae for him."

"But—" Delana hung her head. *I need him to want me.*

"The relationship will work when he comes to you," Mama said firmly. "The two must meet in the middle. It's not for you to go the distance alone."

Yet that's exactly what it feels like. I came so far to be with him, but he can't leave my side fast enough. What am I to do?

"Be patient, Ana." Mama's advice was hard to hear.

"And meanwhile, keep working alongside him in spirit." Gilda began gathering dishes to clean. "Warm smiles with hot meals win men's hearts."

"I'd best be careful, then." Delana smiled wryly. "I only want Dustin's."

"And you'll get it." Mama began helping Gilda. "But for now, there are other things that need your attention."

Delana hurriedly ate a bit of her now-cold corn chowder and nibbled half her biscuit before pitching in. After they'd washed the dishes, they finished up the laundry. The momentous task had taken all of yesterday and most of this morning as well.

The afternoon passed all too quickly as Delana struggled to hasten the pace of the laundry. She scrubbed harder than she'd ever thought possible, dunked garments into the rinse water after boiling, and wrung them as hard as she could. Even so, it was hot, time-consuming work, and she despaired of finishing in time to prepare the grand supper she had in mind.

"You've been working as though the devil himself were cracking the whip." Gilda smoothed back her hair.

"I'd hoped to make a special supper tonight," Delana confessed.

"Rabbit stew?" Gilda suggested. "We baked enough biscuits at lunch to go with it."

"We had corn chowder for dinner, and Irish stew night before last. I hoped to roast the hares and make mashed potatoes"— Delana paused—"and apple cobbler. It's Dustin's favorite."

"I see." Gilda's glance let Delana know she understood exactly what the purpose of this meal was to be. "What do you say to makin' the meal but savin' the cobbler for tomorrow, when we've enough time to do it justice?"

"Sounds like a wonderful plan." She glanced toward Kaitlin and Mama, who hung the last of the laundry. There would still be enough daylight for it all to dry. "I thought that pile would never end!"

"There's some truth in that." Gilda laughed. "But next time we won't have a year's worth of grime to wash out."

"That's the best thing I've heard all day!"

Kaitlin and Mama joined them by the fire. "What are you two plotting up here?"

"Supper." Gilda looked to Delana to explain.

"We thought to roast the rabbits and serve them with mashed potatoes."

"We'll have to try that canned butter then." Mama's tone didn't hide her doubts about the new product.

"I'm sure it'll do just fine." Kaitlin wiped her hands on her apron. "I'll just start those potatoes."

"I'll go get the spit." Delana retrieved the apparatus and set it up with Gilda's help.

"We can't use the bottle jack to turn the meat—there are too many we need to roast at once." Gilda set the hand-turned spit into place. "It's good we thought to bring more than one kind. Now we need to skin those rabbits."

"I've only seen you do that, not tried it myself." Delana tried not to grimace at the grisly prospect.

"I'll skin the first one so you get the idea." With that, she hung the first rabbit above the hock, placing a basin under it, and set to work. After the bleeding, careful skinning, and dressing, the rabbit was ready to cook.

Pushing back a wave of nausea, Delana imitated Gilda's actions. She tried to carefully remove the skin from the meat, only to find the task far messier and much more difficult than it had seemed. By the time Delana finished preparing her first rabbit, Gilda had finished two more.

"You'll improve with practice," the cook encouraged her

after a sidelong glance at the decidedly mangled pelt Delana presented. "By the time we butcher hogs in the fall, you'll be an old hand at things like this."

Delana forced a cheery nod. *I'll prove to Dustin that I'm ready to be here. There are many things I can do to aid my husband-to-be. The first time is always the most difficult whenever I try something new. Dressing game will get easier.*

They alternated between basting the meat and rotating the spit for even roasting. As they worked, Mama boiled the cleaned, peeled potatoes for mashing. Since Rawhide indicted her, Mama had made an impressive effort to do her share.

It's good for her. For both of us, really. It takes our time and keeps us from thinking about lost love. Papa left this world physically, and Dustin has distanced his heart. In Baltimore, we'd be in mourning, but here we have purpose.

Delana watched eagerly as Dustin took his first bite of the roast rabbit. She ignored the approving grunts of the other men in anticipation.

"Mmmmmmm." He closed he eyes as though to prolong the taste.

"I'm so glad you like it!" Delana beamed.

"It's delicious." His smile warmed her until he turned it to Gilda. "Gilda's cooking has always been excellent."

Gilda! Delana fought to keep the smile on her face.

"Delana's as much to thank as I am." Gilda nodded encouragingly. "It was her idea to roast them instead of make a stew."

"Good idea." Dustin barely spared her a glance. "I saw the skins drying—you obviously took great care with them, Gilda. Don't be so modest."

"Ah, but Delana skinned and dressed nearly as many as I did," Gilda explained. "She's a talented cook."

"I see." Dustin swallowed visibly, and Delana watched in dismay as he put his fork down.

❧

Dustin's appetite dwindled as he imagined Delana skinning the rabbits. *I should have skinned and dressed them myself. I was in such a hurry to work on the house that I ruined my gesture. Instead of making this evening meal easier for her, I made her work harder.*

"I should have taken care of it myself." Dustin frowned at the sumptuous meal, now a vivid reminder of how he'd once again failed his bride.

"Why? We're capable of handling it." Delana's chin was raised. "I know I wrote to you about how I cooked with Gilda."

"Of course!" Dustin belatedly realized he'd offended her and tried to clarify. "I just assumed you learned in a real kitchen, with a fancy stove and such."

"Fire is fire," Delana gave a slight huff. "And game and fowl need be dressed before cooking no matter where that fire is."

But it would have been easier for you if I'd thought to do it myself. Even better, if you had a stove and such to work on.

"The house will be ready before you know it." He stuffed more food into his mouth so he wouldn't have to say more.

"We see you work day in and day out." Mrs. Albright bustled up. "You men have many log piles there."

"Yes, you do." Delana seemed to soften with the reminder of how much work he'd put into building their home. "How's it coming?"

"We've hewn and stripped enough trees and taken them to the building site. We're nearly finished peeling the bark so there will be a snug fit between the logs." He finished with pride, "Your summer oven is ready now."

"How wonderful!" Delana's delighted smile made him sit a bit straighter.

"We couldn't work so fast had you not enlisted the labor of the freight drivers," he complimented her. "And the lumber in the freight wagons will be more than enough for a raised floor and loft." He watched as her eyes took on a pleased sparkle. *Good, she deserves to know that her forethought eased the way for both of us.*

"And Isaac is awfully proud about his outhouse." Arthur sounded amused. "We've been sure to let him know how much we appreciate his efforts."

"Don't be forgettin' my Cade installed the new pump." Gilda rested her head on her husband's shoulder. "Laundry will be far simpler next time!"

"I'd say that in three days you ladies will be sleeping in a real house," Dustin ventured.

"Well. . ." Delana's hesitation made the back of Dustin's neck prickle.

Does she not have faith that I'll provide well for her and our family? Have I not shown how far I'll go to give her all I can? When I say it shall be done in three days, I mean it!

"What?" Dustin's voice sounded tight even to him.

"Gilda and I were thinkin' that it would be worth extra time to have everything we'll need." Delana's words sparked his ire.

"Of course you'll have everything you need," he gritted. "Just tell me what it is."

"A root cellar. Gilda and I have read how animals can burrow into a family's root cellar and eat everything they put up!" Delana's brow furrowed with worry. "We wondered if it wouldn't be wisest to dig the root cellar below the house, so there'd be less of a chance that would happen. It would be easier to access come winter, too."

"Ah." Dustin relaxed a bit. "I see you've given this some thought. The reason we wouldn't build a root cellar beneath the house itself is that it makes the cabin more difficult to heat in winter. A large, cold space directly beneath the house would compound a harsh season."

"That makes sense." Delana seemed disappointed. "So what will we do?"

"When we dig out the root cellar, we'll line it with stones to block burrowers." Dustin smiled. "We'll have plenty of stones after clearing our fields." Jakob and Arthur chuckled at that.

"Enough for a smokehouse, too?" Gilda's question gave him pause.

"We dug a cairn near the barn. That saw us through the past winter." Dustin rubbed his jaw. "But we'll need a smokehouse this time around. We'll see to it." He looked at the ladies speculatively. "You've done a lot of thinking about storing provisions. Is there anything else you'll need?"

"We can hang the milk and such in the stream to keep cool, so we don't need a springhouse," Gilda decided. "So there's nothing else that's a necessity."

"A root cellar and smokehouse to join the outdoor oven." Dustin looked to where the freight drivers were already bedding down for a good night's sleep. He'd hoped to raise two cabins while they had the extra hands, and who knew how long Rawhide would stick around?

We'll have the cabin in three days. They've already been here two, and there will be two Lord's days, as well. If we raise another cabin in four days—with Isaac and Cade helping it should be quicker the second time around—we'll have three more days' labor. I need at least one day to help catch up on plowing and planting. In two days we could dig the root cellar and build the smokehouse with so many hands to share the work.

"We'll see to it." He announced his decision.

And we'll take a day between the cabins to build Delana's root cellar. It will be used immediately. I want her to know that her needs are a priority. With God's help, I'll always see them well met.

eight

The next morning, Delana rose bright and early. She'd slept better than she had in weeks.

Good morning, Lord! I want to share my joy with You. I confess that when I first arrived and Dustin seemed so cold, I struggled not to lose heart. He inhaled his food and walked away from me when I yearned for closeness. Last night, when he stopped eating because I'd dressed the rabbits, my heart sank. I thought he didn't believe in me, couldn't imagine me as capable of the tasks I'll need to assume as a farmer's wife. But the more we spoke, the better I felt. Dustin listened to me and asked for my opinions. Finally, we're beginning to work together as I'd thought we would as soon as I arrived. I should have waited patiently on Your time, Lord. I know things will be better now. Thank You for Your many blessings!

After her morning time with God, Delana began her chores. She had all three dairy cows milked before she heard the other women stirring. Delana walked with a light step to build up the cook fire and start the coffee.

"Mornin'." Gilda was the first to join her. "And what were you fixin' to make for breakfast?"

"Have we enough biscuits to just make gravy?" Delana thought of the fresh milk she'd just put in the stream to keep cool. It would taste wonderful after warm gravy on flaky biscuits.

"We've only the canned butter, and we'd best save that."

Gilda rummaged among their supplies. "Bread pudding takes no butter and would taste a treat. I've only ever made it with bread, not biscuits, but I don't see why it won't work."

"Perfect!" Delana started cutting the leftover biscuits into small squares while Gilda pumped and heated water.

They coated the pudding dishes with lard, added the squares to be moistened, and turned their attention toward mixing the batter.

"I'll fetch the milk and eggs." Delana headed for the stream, leaving Gilda to measure out the vanilla and sugar. Returning, she saw Kaitlin and Mama had come out just in time to help dole out the mixture and pop the puddings into the Dutch ovens.

While they baked, some of the men mucked out the barn, while others worked to finish peeling the logs. By the time the puddings had cooled and Delana set out fresh cream, everyone was ready to eat.

Dustin said grace. "Dear Lord, we thank You for the food that smells so good." He took an appreciative sniff before continuing, "And for the able hands who prepared it. We ask that You keep watch over us as we do the work You've given us. Amen."

Delana watched happily as the men, led by Dustin, made short work of their breakfasts. Her joy increased when he stopped beside her before going to work.

"Today we'll notch the logs and build the foundation." He patted her on the shoulder, giving her a smile before he moved on.

Dustin's bit of attention caused Delana to hum later as she washed dishes alongside the other women. "We'll be able to bake real bread today," she all but sang the words. "Dustin told me the summer oven is ready."

"We must churn butter." Mama looked to the rope holding the buckets of milk in the cool water.

"We'll need it to make apple cobbler." Delana stacked the dishes and carried them back.

With that, they settled into the same routine they'd used two days ago, working alongside one another to speed the process.

"I still canna believe we've gone through so many biscuits in two days!" Kaitlin pinched some dough into shape after they'd been working awhile.

"We'll make enough loaves of bread to last three." Gilda put the first four loaves in the ovens.

"We filled each oven five times over before." Delana waited for the next batch of dough to rise. "So this time we'll do seven. . .no, eight would be best."

"Aye, best finish it all at once." Kaitlin dusted some flour off her apron. "When the cabin's up, we'll need to spend our time planting a good-sized garden."

"With the way Rawhide eats, we'll have to plant double!" The small smile on Mama's face belied her words.

"I was under the impression he decided to lend a hand while we were in need." Gilda headed toward the fire.

"I hadn't thought of that." Mama stopped mixing for a moment then stirred more forcefully. "That'll save us some work."

"Don't be so sure." Delana hadn't missed the flicker in her mother's eyes. Rough though he was, Rawhide had pulled Mama out of her deep grief and made her concentrate on the present. "I've no doubt he'll be a frequent visitor. Where else can he get so much good food?"

"He is a wily one," Gilda chuckled.

They settled into the rhythm of baking, and by the time Gilda pulled the last golden-brown loaves out of the ovens, they needed to start dinner.

It's a lot of work, Delana admitted to herself as she re-pinned a few errant wisps of her hair, *but there's satisfaction to be found in a job well done and pleasure in good company. I might even miss the way we cook out here once the house is up.*

≈

Once the house is up, they'll be able to cook over a stove the way ladies should. Dustin finished notching the first end of his umpteenth log. I'll build a large table the same day we dig the root cellar. Delana will lack for nothing.

"Eleven pairs of hands make this go fast." Jakob took a swig of water from his canteen. "We'll be finished by dinnertime."

"I hope so." Dustin looked around and saw that his future brother-in-law was right. They were working at a mighty pace. "We'll be able to lay the foundation and floorboards this afternoon, with time to spare."

"If all goes this well tomorrow," Cade fanned himself with his hat as he joined the conversation, "we'll have the cabin up and sealed with a day to spare."

"Not quite." Dustin wiped his hands on his bandana. "The roof joists will take some time, as will the loft inside. Any time left over should be put to helping the ladies settle in."

"We sure brought enough stuff to haul in." Isaac swiped a hand across his forehead.

"If you keep shootin' the breeze," Rawhide grunted from a

short ways behind them, "we'll never get this thing up."

Dustin didn't speak with anyone again until the final log was fully peeled and notched.

"Good job," he congratulated them all. He was just beginning to wonder whether they had enough time to begin the foundation before—

"Dinner!" They all heard the bell and took off at the same time.

The warm, yeasty scent of fresh-baked bread tickled Dustin's nose long before he reached the table. After he said the blessing, he swallowed spoonfuls of the savory chicken broth, using a third piece of the soft, pillowy bread to soak up what his spoon couldn't reach.

He sighed with satisfaction when he'd finished and patted his stomach. When Delana came to collect his bowl, she giggled.

"What's so funny?" He handed her his spoon, too.

"The way you're sighing and holding your stomach, anyone would think you had a tummy ache but for the pleased grin on your face."

"A good midday meal after a hard morning's work is more than worth appreciating." He stood up.

"It's good to hear you say that." The quiet pleasure in her voice caught his attention.

"Why?"

"You've all but inhaled your food at every meal then hurried away again just as fast."

"I wanted to keep on schedule building our home," he explained. "My rush never meant I didn't enjoy what you put on the table."

"I wasn't sure." Her admission felt like a punch in the gut.

For a year I put my heart and soul into clearing the land she stands upon. I was to have thirteen more months to see to the niceties, yet she arrives far in advance. By attempting to rectify our lack of a house, she feels as though I'm not letting her know I appreciate her. Every single thing I do is to provide for our family, but she somehow interprets it as neglect. What more am I to do?

"Now that you are sure I like the cooking, I've got to get back to work." He jammed his hat on his head and stalked back to the building site.

In the heat of the afternoon, they swiftly built the foundation and affixed the wooden floor he knew Delana would want. A dirt floor couldn't be kept clean and invited bugs into the home—an unpleasant truth he and the guys had discovered out in the barn.

When that was done, they all took a moment to admire their handiwork and drink some water. The sun had not even begun to set, so they had a couple good work hours left to begin building the house.

"Let's divide up into pairs," Dustin directed. "It'll take four two-man teams to maneuver the logs into place." He joined up with Rawhide, Jakob with Arthur, and the freight drivers paired up as they had when sawing the trees. Dustin turned to Cade and Isaac. "We'll be needing the pulley system for the higher logs. You're both good at that sort of thing—why don't you rig it up until one of the men needs to be relieved?"

"Sure." They headed off to get some rope.

Privately, Dustin was glad they wouldn't be called upon to lift the heavy logs. *Cade's older than Rawhide but not used to life out here. Isaac is young but overeager and not yet at full growth. Either of them could easily hurt himself with this kind of work, and*

I'm thankful for the other things they can accomplish more safely. Not that he'd ever tell either one—it'd be insulting.

By the time they'd laid the first six rows of logs, fitting them by the notches in the corners, Dustin had reason to praise their progress.

"We'll try to finish this stage before noon tomorrow. That way, we'll not be doing the hardest work in the heat of the day." His announcement was met with fervent agreement from all the men.

"We have it ready!" Isaac and Cade showed the clever pulley system they'd set up. "It's counterweighted so the logs won't tip it over," Isaac explained.

"It'll be a great help from here on out," Dustin approved. The thought of hefting logs any higher than they'd already managed made his back twinge. The walls already stood as tall as his head, and they each needed another five logs if there was to be room for a loft.

"Progress will be slower tomorrow," Jakob assessed.

"Perhaps not." Dustin grinned. "Isaac and Cade's hoisting system will speed things up. I'm sure we'll finish the basics tomorrow." *And in another day, Delana will have a real home.*

nine

"It's amazing how much you've done," Delana perched next to Dustin on a boulder by the barn.

"Just wait until tomorrow." Pure masculine contentment underlay each word. "We'll have it up entirely."

"We'll be moving in tomorrow night?" Delana jumped up in excitement.

"No." His curt tone made her stiffen. "The structure will be up, complete with roof and loft, but there won't be time to settle in until after the next day."

"Let me fetch some dessert. While we enjoy it, you can tell me exactly what else needs to be done." She couldn't imagine what more would complete their house. She walked over to where Gilda was already dishing up the fragrant cobblers. Delana grabbed a dish. "This should have them smiling," she reveled.

"You and your beau seemed quite cozy whilst you ate your supper." Gilda dished up a chunk and kept repeating the action as she spoke. "Why don't you take these two plates and relax a bit? Kaitlin's comin' to help me pass these out."

"I don't think it will be too difficult to find the recipients." Delana tilted her head to where Isaac and Arthur were already edging near. Laughing, Gilda shooed her back to Dustin's side.

"Here you are." Delana presented the treat to Dustin with a flourish.

"Apple cobbler!" Dustin clutched the plate greedily. "I

thought I was imagining the scent!" He breathed in the sweet cinnamon aroma before taking a bite. "Mmmmmm. . ."

"It is pretty good," Delana judged after sampling her own piece.

"Best thing I've tasted in a year," Dustin said fervently. "I didn't know you brought apples."

"Of course I brought some! I know apple cobbler is your favorite."

Dustin paused between bites long enough to mention, "Except for apple pie."

Delana laughed. "Or any type of apple dessert."

"I'll never say no to an apple." Dustin savored the last bite of his dessert before eyeing her plate speculatively.

"Here." Delana switched their plates to give him the last morsel. "But supposedly, thinking that way got Adam into trouble."

"Oh no, you don't." Dustin would have looked dignified if it weren't for the flake of crust on his chin. "The Bible never says it was an apple." He waved his fork at her. "Don't malign the fruit unless you have the facts."

"Fair enough." Delana stacked the plates but stayed beside him. "So what do you plan to do after tomorrow?"

"We need to cut out areas for windows and the door, install both, and then seal the walls." He paused. "Otherwise it will provide precious little protection from wind and rain."

"I see what you mean." She realized the gaps between the logs needed filling. Delana put a hand on his warm forearm. "You've thought of everything."

"That's what Isaac, Cade, and Rawhide say of you." Dustin chuckled. "It was good thinking to bring along the cut lumber and bricks for the summer oven."

"But not the windows?" She arched a brow.

"They'll let in light and make our home more cheerful." He paused. "But it would be foolish to install all the panes you've brought."

"Why?" She withdrew her hand and frowned. Packing the glass had been even more difficult than packing fresh eggs in barrels of cornmeal.

"Large windows put us at risk—they're too easy for a bear to crash through."

"Oh." Delana shuddered at the image he painted. "How small will they be?"

"Four panes per window." Dustin held his arms in the air to demonstrate the size. "We'll put one on either side of the door."

"What of the other walls?" She didn't have a clear picture as to what their home would look like from the inside.

"The far wall"—Dustin gestured left—"will have a loft coming halfway into the cabin. It will sleep Gilda and Kaitlin now, and someday. . ."

"Children," Delana breathed. *He's thought of our babies, too!* The thought elated her.

"You and Mama Albright will sleep in the nook underneath." He paused, cleared his throat, but didn't say what Delana knew they were both thinking.

"What of the kitchen?" She eased the awkwardness.

"We'll put the stove in the far right corner." Dustin framed the area with his hands as he spoke. "I'll build shelves on the wall beside it, and a sturdy table and benches, too."

"You don't want windows near the beds or stove, so the house will remain warm even in the dead of winter." Delana came to the conclusion slowly. "Well, I brought enough glass for three times that." She smiled at his astonishment. "Mama doesn't know, but I brought extra so she and Jakob could enjoy the light, as well. The Bannings brought enough for one window in their cabin and in Arthur and Kaitlin's."

"Even so, there will still be gracious plenty left." Dustin looked out at the fire. "When we build homes for the Bannings and Arthur and Kaitlin, we'll put them to use."

"What a wonderful idea!" Delana tucked a lock of hair behind her ear. "Each of their homes can have two windows, just as ours will!"

"That's more than they planned on," Dustin observed.

"I like that idea far more than extra windows in our own home." Delana turned to him. "Can we keep it a secret until the time comes?"

"As a surprise?" He flashed a conspiratorial grin. "They'd enjoy it even more that way."

"And so will we." She reached her hand toward his, sighing softly when he wrapped it in his. His warm smile warded off the chill of the deepening night. "So will we."

❧

With her sweet little hand nestled softly in his own, far larger, rougher one, Dustin resolved once again to protect her. *Her hands aren't as soft as they were in Baltimore.* He rubbed his thumb across her palm and smiled when he felt her slight shiver.

It amazed him how much these delicate hands had taken on since she arrived. *She doesn't stand over a stove to cook; instead she labors over heavy pots in an open fire. The meat here doesn't come from a butcher, neatly skinned and dressed, but from our own land.*

In Baltimore, she had Gilda to cook for her. She learned in order to prepare herself for life on a farm. Delana packed everything up and led her family across civilized America to join me in the wilds of the frontier.

"You've done well." He stood up, pulling her to her feet. "It's cold out here, and we've more than earned a night's rest."

"Good night, Dustin." She stood very close, her hand still in his. Her eyes, large and luminous in the moonlight, seemed vulnerable. The chill reddened her cheeks, and he could see the faint mist of her breath between slightly parted lips.

It would be so easy to slide my arm around her back, take one step closer, and kiss her. He struggled with the impulse. *She's just lost her father. It's been a long, hard day, and she blushed when I spoke of the sleeping arrangements.* He forced himself to step away from the woman he loved. *My fiancée deserves my respect and understanding.*

"Good night, Delana." As she walked away, he went to make his bed on the cold, hard ground.

When he awoke the next morning, Dustin stretched before scooting out from under the freight wagon. The first night he'd slept out here, he'd sat up too fast and cracked his head.

He pulled on his boots, scratched his prickly jaw, and realized no one else was awake yet. After giving serious consideration to lying back down for a little more shut-eye, he tugged on his boots, grabbed his razor, and took off for the stream. After cupping some of the fresh water to his lips, he looked around at the quiet beauty of the morning.

Lord, You've helped us accomplish more than I dared hope we could in a short period of time. Thank You for that. I ask for Your guiding hand as we finish the cabin today, and that all of the men remain safe. Amen.

He got off his knees and began walking to the barn before he realized he couldn't start mucking out the stalls—not while the women still slept inside. Dustin turned his attention toward the cabin but knew he couldn't lift the heavy logs on his own.

Some of the ends of the logs, left over from when they cut the beams to size, caught his eye. He strode to them and began comparing the sections too thin for the eighteen-foot-long walls. After much consideration, he selected four thick branches, each roughly three feet tall. He braced the longer one, marked it, and began to saw down the others to make table legs. When he had the four sections even, he stopped and checked to see what everyone else was doing.

The women were stirring—Delana had already toted pails of milk to the stream. The men had risen, as well. Cade and Isaac stood testing the ropes of their hoist. Dustin set aside the wood. He planned to make supports for the kitchen table out of the sturdy logs, but for now he needed to go about the morning tasks.

As soon as all four women were out of the barn, he and Jakob mucked it out and replaced the soiled hay with fresh. They found Rawhide overseeing the men; Isaac and Cade strapped the selected log into the ropes while the other men prepared to pull them taut. Dustin and Jakob hurried over to watch the log be lifted quickly and smoothly.

"Ease up!" Rawhide directed as the log swung high into the air—far too high for its intended placement. The men slowly fed back a length of the rope until the log hung over its mates. Dustin and Jakob each held an end of the notched log and fitted it into place before detaching the ropes.

"It works!" Isaac puffed out his chest.

"Let's get another one ready." Dustin helped wrestle the next log into the rope harness. In a remarkably short period of time, they'd laid the seventh layer of the walls before the breakfast bell rang.

Dustin found himself gobbling his oatmeal as though he'd not eaten in months. *You've all but inhaled your food at every meal and hurried away again just as fast.* Delana's quiet words echoed in his mind, and he set aside his impatience to linger over the morning meal.

Delana kept busy pouring milk and wouldn't meet his gaze. He didn't have so much as a chance to smile at her before the other men were putting down their bowls and looking to Dustin. He drew on his work gloves and led them back to the cabin. There, he became distracted from Delana's strange behavior as the cabin grew before their eyes.

The joists took longer, as did the rafters and support beams for the roof. One false move would be disastrous with the angled slope. Using the ladders from the barn, they finished the paneling for the roof. The bark peeled from the logs created rough shingles that the men nailed into place.

"We've come a long way." Jakob clapped a hand on Dustin's shoulder.

"After dinner we'll measure and cut out segments for the door and windows," Dustin planned aloud. "At this rate, we'll have all of them installed before the night's out."

"Good." Arthur came to stand beside them. "This will be the last night my wife and babe sleep in a tack room."

"Yes." Dustin took a deep breath. "It's good to be ahead of schedule." *For the first time since Delana arrived, things are within my control.*

ten

"Kaitlin!" Delana watched in horror as her friend tripped. Kaitlin curled around her baby as she hit the earth. Delana reached her side a moment too late.

"Ro—sa—lind," Kaitlin panted, the air knocked from her lungs.

"It'll be all right." *Lord, please let her be all right.* Delana took the crying baby and unwrapped her blanket. She felt the soft down of Rosalind's head before gently probing chubby arms and legs. "No bumps or broken bones," she told Kaitlin as Rosalind began to suck her thumb.

"Praise the Lord." Kaitlin winced as she sat up. Bracing herself on one hand, she peered at the ground. "I stepped in a gopher hole."

"Don't get up!" Delana shifted the baby over her shoulder.

"Let me take a look at you," Gilda clucked over her daughter. She pushed Kaitlin's skirt up to press on her daughter's ankle. When pain made her hiss out a breath, Gilda resigned herself to the worst. "We'd best take your shoe off afore it isn't possible." She set about undoing the laces of Kaitlin's half boot.

"I've just wrenched it." Kaitlin tried to stand up again.

"Where did you fall?" Mama put out a hand to stop her.

"Right here." Kaitlin sounded confused.

"No, no." Mama tried again. "What part of you fell?"

"I wrenched my ankle and pretty much went sprawling, so. . . all of me, I suppose."

"She means what part hit the ground first," Delana clarified. Mama usually had no trouble with English, but occasionally she'd arrange the words as though it were German.

"I twisted to shield Rosalind, so this shoulder." Kaitlin gestured to her left. "Ouch!"

Mama gently pressed around the area, and soon it was evident that more than Kaitlin's ankle was bruised.

"Here." Delana slid the baby into Gilda's arms and looped Kaitlin's right arm around her shoulders. Soon, Kaitlin was standing on her good ankle, and Delana supported her as they hobbled back to the barn.

Mama fetched the medicine bag and followed. Using some cool water from the stream, she fashioned cold compresses.

"You rest awhile." Gilda smoothed back her daughter's hair. "We'll leave Rosalind with you, and maybe you can both sleep a bit. I'll wrap the ankle in a while."

"Not that I have much choice," Kaitlin commented wryly as she lay down.

"Try to enjoy the chance to take it easy." Delana winked at her. "Praise God it wasn't more serious."

"Amen to that." Gilda clasped her hands together.

"Ana, why don't you stay with Katie?" Mama said.

"It's about time to start dinner," she pointed out.

"Gilda and I can handle making the potato soup." Mama put her hands on her hips. "We've a ready supply of fresh milk and plenty of butter after yesterday afternoon. Surely we can boil some potatoes without you two."

"Don't forget all the bread we baked yesterday morning." Gilda nodded. "You two can chat awhile. If you want to keep yourselves busy, that pile of mending might call to you."

"I'll just fetch our sewing boxes and be right back." Delana traipsed out to the wagon and rummaged around until she found the two wooden boxes. *Soon, all our things will be in our house—not out here in these old wagons.*

"Socks or shirts?" Delana began pulling items from the pile. "It's amazing how hard these men have been on their poor clothes."

"Always have been." Kaitlin laughed. "I'll take the socks. Arthur mentioned he hadn't gotten but one pair back after washday, so I'd wager most of these are his."

"Don't be so sure." Delana poked a finger through a hole in the toe of one sock and waggled it, much to Rosalind's delight. "There are far more here than one man could claim."

"Then we'd best get to it. Blisters put a man in a sore disposition." The two women threaded their needles and began darning.

"There's hardly any sock left to this one!" Delana held up one with more holes than fabric.

Kaitlin sighed. "Put it in the rag pile."

"What's the matter?" Delana stopped stitching and looked at her friend in concern. "Do you hurt?"

"The ankle twinges," she admitted, "but 'tis my pride botherin' me most."

"It could have happened to any one of us. We all cross the meadow several times a day." Delana patted Katie's knee. "No need to fret."

"Yet I'm the only one who managed to take a tumble." Kaitlin gave a rueful smile. "The men fell trees and lift the logs all day, coming back with nothing more damaging then a few splinters."

"Thank God they're all hale and well." Delana resumed stitching. "But I'll venture to say none of the men go about their tasks while carrying a spirited babe."

"True enough." Katie brightened and picked up a sock. "Rosalind can be a handful. Ma says she has my mischief."

"She'll need it." Delana looked at the babe. "It takes courage and grit to live here."

"In the wilderness, or outnumbered by men?" Katie wondered aloud.

"Both!" They shared a laugh before a contented silence fell. Too soon, Delana's thoughts turned to Dustin.

Last night we spoke and laughed like we used to. When we said good night, I thought I saw a gleam in his eyes. . . but he didn't kiss me. I'm his wife-to-be. Why does he shy away?

"What has you frownin' so?" Katie had stopped darning to watch her face.

"Nothing of any great import." Delana tried to shrug off her unease.

"Oh no, you don't. You canna listen to my frettin' over a turned ankle and dismiss whatever causes you worry." Kaitlin gave her an arched look. "Out with it."

"It—it's of a personal nature," Delana murmured.

"So it has to do with Dustin, does it? I thought you two looked cozy last night, yet you didn't go near him this morn."

"He talked to me of how he'd build our home, and what it would look like inside. I hadn't felt so close to him since Baltimore." Delana tied off the last stitch and put down another sock.

"But. . ." Katie coaxed. "Don't be lookin' surprised. 'Tis obvious that's not the end of it."

"When everyone was busy getting ready for bed, he took my hand and held it in his." Delana remembered the reassuring warmth of his strong clasp. "He stood up, pulling me with him. It seemed like such a right moment, with the moonlight shining through the leaves and our hands still linked. . ."

"The right moment for a bit of affection, you mean." Katie smiled. "You're engaged, soon to be man and wife, and reunited after a long absence. 'Tis only natural."

"My thoughts were much the same as he looked into my eyes and stood so close. . .but he stepped back and said good night." Hurt welled up at the memory. "I thought we were past his disappointment at my early arrival—which was awkward enough—but now I wonder if he wants me to wife." The words came in a rush, as though they couldn't be true if she spoke them quickly enough.

"Now then, you might be confused about him pulling away, but don't doubt he wants you." Kaitlin leaned forward intently. "No man works every minute of the day to build a house for a woman he doesna love."

"Yet it wasn't until last night we managed to spend any time together at all. It's as though he's too busy. . ."

"It's his way of showing he intends to provide for ye. Look at the works of his hands as though they were sweet words."

"It would be easier to do so if he held me close instead of pushing me away." To her horror, her eyes grew misty.

Kaitlin spoke slowly, tactfully. "Had you ever shared a kiss before he set off for the frontier?"

"Twice, once when we became engaged and again on the

day he left." Delana's cheeks flushed at the memory of his strong arms around her, his warm lips pressed against hers in silent promise.

"Wait." Kaitlin's voice pulled Delana from her reverie. "You've been apart an entire year, with naught but letters to bind your hearts. He knows you're grieving the loss of your father and brother. . .he honors you by taking it slowly."

"Perhaps." Delana turned back to her mending, but her thoughts grew more tumultuous. *But perhaps I'd rather be loved than honored.*

❧

"Where's Delana?" Dustin squinted but didn't see her anywhere when he answered the dinner bell.

"And Katie?" Arthur wondered.

Gilda wiped her hands on her apron. "They're in the barn after a wee accident this morn—"

Dustin took off toward the barn before she finished and knew from the thundering footsteps behind him that Arthur had the same idea. Dustin paused to open the barn door when they reached it, and Arthur rushed past him.

"Katie!" he bellowed, kneeling and gathering his wife to his chest.

"Delana?" Dustin rushed to her side but didn't see anything amiss as his fiancée dropped her mending in surprise.

"Yes, Dustin?" Her brow crinkled as she looked at Arthur hugging Kaitlin close.

"Gilda said there was an accident." Dustin peered at Delana intently, his gaze taking stock from the crown of her head to the soles of her dainty shoes. "Are you all right?"

"I'm fine, and so is Kaitlin." Delana raised her voice and

added, "Though that was before a blacksmith came in to smother her."

"Ease up," Dustin cautioned Arthur as one glance showed Delana's assessment to be true. In his relief, the burly blacksmith had pressed his wife to his chest so tightly Kaitlin could hardly draw breath.

"What happened?" Dustin demanded, willing his heart to beat at a normal pace. When he thought Delana was hurt, he'd been all but unable to breathe himself.

"Kaitlin took a spill today," she calmly explained. "She had the quick wits to curl around Rosalind so the baby wasn't hurt."

"I stepped in a gopher hole and turned my ankle." Kaitlin ducked her head in embarrassment.

"And here it is, wrapped up tight wi' you sitting to gie it a rest." Arthur gave a deep sigh of relief. " 'Tis thankful I am you suffered no worse."

"She'll have a bright bruise on her shoulder as well." Delana's news made the churning in Dustin's guts grow worse. "But she'll be fine, and the baby has no injuries. A few days rest"— she broke off to share a grin with Kaitlin—"while we finish all your mending will see her put to rights."

"That's my girl." Arthur gave Kaitlin's uninjured shoulder one last squeeze before rising to his feet. "I'll bring you and Delana some dinner so you don't have to stir yourselves." He grinned at Delana. "I trust you to see to it she gets in no more trouble."

"I make no promises."

Dustin scowled darkly as he and Arthur left the barn. *I was a fool to think I had things in hand.*

"Quit your glowerin'." Arthur stopped walking after glimpsing Dustin's expression. "All is as well as it can be—spilled milk and all o' that."

"Hardly. Kaitlin could have harmed a lot more than her ankle when she fell. What if she had hit her head on a stone, or the babe took most of the impact?"

"The Lord was watchin' o'er my wife and child this morn," Arthur agreed. "It does Him no service to dwell on the evil He didn't let befall us."

"Open your eyes!" Dustin squared his shoulders. "This was nothing less than a solemn warning. Women and children do not belong out here—it's far too dangerous."

"I wouldn't go so far." Arthur frowned.

"I would. What if it had been a snake hole? A single angry bite and we could have lost either of them." Dustin crossed his arms. "And that is from a mere stumble. At any moment, they could walk beneath an old tree and be crushed by a widow-maker. Remember the day they first arrived and we worried a bear came to challenge our claim? There are mountain lions, too. We're not so far into warm weather that a snap blizzard couldn't destroy us. Remember the June freeze Rawhide told us about?"

" 'Twas a year afore we e'en arrived. You're dealin' in ifs, Dustin."

"A man has to," he responded grimly. "Any one of a dozen things could harm our women out here—and we don't control a single one of them." The very thought made his blood run cold.

"Then what do you suggest? We keep them bundled up in the barn for now and locked inside the house once it's finished?" Arthur scoffed. "Life on the frontier is an adventure we knew Kaitlin and Delana would share with us sooner or later."

"Later, after we had a house, when we could be close to them more often and be on hand should the need arise." Dustin clenched his hands into fists at his sides. "Like today."

"We'll have the first house tomorrow," Arthur pointed out. "If that's what troubles you, 'twill na be an issue for long."

"And the baby? The wilderness is no place for an infant." Dustin shook his head. "They shouldn't be here."

"They're our women. Of course they should be here."

"No. We're honor bound to protect them, and right now we've too much to accomplish." Dustin took a deep breath before announcing his decision. "They must go back."

eleven

"Dinna be daft, man!" Arthur rolled his eyes.

"I'm not." Dustin tugged his hat brim lower on his forehead.

"You most certainly are, makin' a mountain outta a gopher hole," Arthur scoffed. "There are gopher holes anywhere."

"Think, Arthur!" Dustin had to talk some sense into the burly blacksmith. "It's the least of the perils here."

"Aye, so I canna fathom why you're bent sideways o'er it."

"They've scarcely been here for three days, and already Kaitlin is injured. The babe would easily have been harmed, as well."

"Anything that pains my wife pains my heart." Arthur's brow furrowed. "I'm that sorry her ankle hurts her, but such a thing isna so dire as to take her from my side."

Dustin jumped on his words. "The next thing could be. So many things could cost a life."

"I dinna mean her passin' on," Arthur growled. "I referred to your cockamamie plan of sendin' them away. I lived without my wife for a year, and I wouldn't bear her absence again after so short a reprieve."

"Isn't it worth missing them if it keeps them safe?" Dustin kept pressing. *Next it could be worse. Next time it could be Delana.*

"Nay, you've the wrong of it. 'Twas na right to leave my wife 'tall, but 'twas necessary. I missed the birth of my child."

Arthur crossed massive arms over his barrel of a chest. "I'll not miss Rosalind's early smiles, nor any of the sweet firsts that lie ahead. She'll be crawling, then toddlin' and talkin' to her da in the blink of an eye. I would share those joyous moments with my bonnie Kaitlin."

"But they'd be more secure back in Baltimore."

"How so? They've no home, no business, and no men save Cade, who's now a grandda, and Isaac, who's barely more than a whelp." Arthur gestured to the freight wagons and buckboards to illustrate his next point. "They sold everythin' and spent that money on passage here and supplies to carry us through. Where would you have them go, alone and without means?"

"I. . ." Dustin pondered the situation. *Delana, Isaac, and Mrs. Albright have funds—although it would be like them to pay for the Bannings and Arthur's wife to come. Their home is gone—she gave up everything to come here. How can I turn her away after she's journeyed so far to reach my side? The war rages on, with more battlefields and horrors each day. At least here, she is away from all that.*

The thought of Delana coming into contact with jaded soldiers made his blood run cold. *Which is safer—a civilized place in the midst of a savage war, or a wilderness isolated from human ugliness but full of other dangers?*

Faced with the weight of his lack of options, Dustin heaved a sigh and did the only thing he could. "We'd better eat some dinner and get back to building the cabin."

"Aye." A grin broke out across Arthur's face. "We do what we can and rely on God to o'ersee the rest."

"It's harder than it sounds," Dustin grumbled as they walked toward Gilda's pot.

"Keep faith that the Lord cares for us, and remember"— Arthur cracked his fingers loudly before bestowing his final pearl of wisdom—"The most difficult things can be the most rewarding."

❧

Delana and Kaitlin watched the men leave the barn before bursting into laughter.

"Oh," Kaitlin gasped. "They stampeded in here like panicked cattle!"

"And if Arthur held you any tighter, you would've fainted from lack of breath." Delana's giggles subsided. "It's wonderful to see how much he loves you, rushing in here and holding on like he'd never let go."

"It's a good thing he did!" Kaitlin straightened her skirts. "Did you notice Dustin came running, too? I suppose Mam didn't tell them which one of us was the poor unfortunate."

"Maybe." Delana brightened. The intense gaze Dustin leveled as he looked her up and down had made her breath hitch. He'd made absolutely sure she was all right.

"Why don't you go ahead and help them bring in dinner? I don't think the chances of them carrying all that food without spilling someone's soup are very good."

"You're probably right." Delana headed toward the barn door and found it partly open. She reached to push it fully open but stopped as he heard Dustin's voice ring out.

"We're honor bound to protect them, and right now we've too much to accomplish." There was a brief pause and Delana debated whether to tiptoe away or fling open the door.

"They must go back." Her fiancé's pronouncement stopped her in her tracks.

Is he talking about us? Delana bit her lower lip. *He couldn't possibly be thinking of sending us away!* Panic whirled about her as thickly as the dust motes dancing in the sunlight. As she stood frozen in shock, the men kept talking.

Daft is right! She silently applauded Arthur as he told Dustin that he was "makin' a mountain outta a gopher hole." The phrase made her smile, but the meaning broke her heart as the man she loved argued to send her packing.

The difference between Dustin's line of thinking and Arthur's stalwart defense of his wife's presence staggered Delana. *Dustin wants me as far away as possible, but Kaitlin's husband fights for the privilege of having her by his side. Why can't Dustin feel that way about me?*

Afraid to move for fear of their hearing her, she cried silently as Arthur passionately declared he would share the joyous moments of life with Kaitlin. Even in the face of such devotion, Dustin never stopped pressing to have his way.

Lord, I let myself believe Dustin loved me and wanted me to wife. Here he is, turning away from me in the face of something so small as a wrenched ankle. The love between a man and a woman is to be as Your love for us—a thing pure and strong in spite of the obstacles we face. Dustin speaks of peril and wanting to spare us from danger. Doesn't he realize that his words and actions are the greatest threat to my happiness?

While she sought the Lord's wisdom, Arthur talked sense into Dustin. She finally heard her stubborn man capitulate— but only after Arthur pointed out that there was no home to send her back to. With heavy heart and hunched shoulders, Delana returned to the tack room.

"What happened?" In spite of her ankle, Kaitlin managed

to scramble upright and throw her arms around Delana.

"D–D–Dustin wants to send us away," she blubbered into Kaitlin's collar.

"Over a wrenched ankle?" Her friend's astonishment made it all the worse.

"He's using it as a pretext." Delana's sobs wouldn't stop. "Dustin doesn't want me here. . ."

"Now, I'm sure that's not so." Kaitlin's crooned words held no comfort.

"I heard him and Arthur." She sniffed and tried to stop crying. The men would be back with dinner soon.

"You listened in?" Kaitlin stiffened with disapproval.

"No. I was about to push open the door when I heard Dustin say he'd send us away. After that, I couldn't move. . ." Delana wiped her eyes with the back of her hand. "I kept thinking about how much effort I put into packing, how long the journey was, and how hard I've worked to prove I'm ready. . .all for nothing."

"And is he still set on this foolish plan?"

"Arthur talked some sense into Dustin's thick skull." Delana helped Kaitlin back down to her mattress.

"Then there's no permanent harm done." Katie cocked her head to the side. "Did you hear him say why he wanted us to leave?"

"Something about how gopher holes are the least of the dangers out here and that we'd be safer back home until they were ready to take care of us." Delana glowered at the memory. "As though we're Rosalind's age."

"There, you see? 'Tisna that he doesna want you—'tis that he wants you to be safe." Kaitlin shrugged. "Mam says men oftimes get such silly notions stuck in their heads. We women have to be patient and clever enough to get past it."

"And if I feel neither patient nor clever?" Delana sat back down.

" 'Twill pass. Think on all you've done up to now, Delana." Kaitlin gave her an encouraging smile. "You're plenty clever and certainly capable. We'll just have to ask God's help with the patience."

"And meanwhile? What do I say when Dustin walks back through the door?"

"You thank him for bringing your dinner and smile as prettily as possible." Kaitlin winked. "And I'd mention some of those things you're always saying about how beautiful the mountains are or how the clear blue sky makes you feel as though heaven is nearer to this place than any other. 'Twill put him in mind of the blessings you enjoy here."

"It doesn't sit well to not tell him what I overheard." Delana squirmed. "It seems. . ."

"It seems to me as though the place to protest was by the barn door." Kaitlin leaned close. "Glowerin' at him now willna change anything except prove to him you're unhappy. 'Twould be a different matter were he still set on sending us back, but he's already decided not to. When the time comes, you'll speak with him about the way he's made you feel."

"When the time comes," Delana repeated thoughtfully. Kaitlin's advice made good sense.

"I don't know what time you're talking about"—Dustin's voice preceded him into the tack room—"but the food has come!"

"And plenty of it." Arthur stooped a bit to fit through the doorway.

"Oh my." Delana jumped to her feet and relieved Dustin of two of the hot soup bowls he clutched against his chest. "You're lucky you didn't burn yourself. Who carries four bowls of soup?"

"The man who isn't toting two platters of fresh bread and a crock of butter." Arthur carefully passed the food to Kaitlin before plunking down on the floor.

"I brought the preserves!" Mama came bustling in, and the room seemed very small indeed.

"Mama?"

"Well, I couldn't very well leave two young women alone with two young men in our sleeping quarters!" She seemed shocked by the very thought.

"You forgot Baby Rosalind." Delana gestured to where the child lay beside Kaitlin.

"And that we're already wed," Arthur put his arm around Kaitlin's waist.

"But we're glad to see you," Delana broke in to avert Mama's next comment.

"And the preserves!" Dustin added some to the slice of bread and butter he then passed to Delana.

"I wondered where everyone went." Rawhide shadowed the doorway and looked at the indoor picnic.

"Join us." Mama's invitation surprised Delana, but she held her tongue.

"There's no place for a man like me here."

"Such nonsense." Mama waved away what she probably thought was false modesty. "You asked me to help you with the manners, and I tell you to sit down."

"There's no place for me to sit," Rawhide clarified, eying the slice of bread Arthur was slathering with butter.

"Sit where you stand." Mama held up a thick slice of the warm bread. "Butter?"

"Yeah." Rawhide somehow tucked himself half inside the doorway, half out.

"Yes, please," Mama corrected. She smeared butter and blackberry preserves on the slice and held it just out of reach until Rawhide caught on.

"Yes, please," he echoed plaintively. He stuffed the treat in his mouth almost as soon as he touched it.

"And now what do you say?" Mama was clearly angling for a thank-you.

"Mmmmmff." Rawhide took another huge bite and grunted. "Good."

The men guffawed while Delana and Kaitlin tried to smother their amusement.

"Thank you," Mama corrected.

"You're welcome?" Rawhide seemed to think she was thanking him for the compliment.

"I—" Mama shrugged. "It's a start."

Delana looked at where Dustin sat tickling baby Rosalind. *Dustin's a bit rough, too.* He caught her watching and smiled. *But it's a start.*

twelve

The men hastily fell into line, effectively blocking most of the cabin from view. Dustin stood with his back squarely against the door as the women advanced. He didn't even try to hold back his grin. *Thank You, Lord, for the perfect timing. We finished the loft just as Gilda rang the dinner bell. The cabin is ready for them now.*

"Up you are to things." Mrs. Albright's gaze darted from Jakob to Dustin to Rawhide.

"That means she thinks we're up to something," Jakob translated. "She's always right when she says that."

" 'Tis glad I am we won't disappoint her." Arthur stared fixedly at Kaitlin.

"You have to admit we've never ignored the meal bell before," Dustin gloated. "Since we couldn't bring the cabin to the cooks. . ."

"You brought us to the cabin." Delana reached him first. "After keeping us far away for the past four days, you intentionally ignored the dinner bell." She raised on her tiptoes and craned her neck, trying to see around the line of men. "It'd serve all of you right if your food burned."

"It won't, will it?" Dustin's grin slipped.

"Nay." Gilda chuckled.

"Can we see it or not?" Delana tapped her foot impatiently.

"It's finished." Dustin straightened his shoulders and took a step forward, closing the distance between them. "And you'll be the first to see it." With a sudden move that made her gasp, he swept her into his arms. He tucked in his chin until his forehead touched hers and rumbled as quietly as he could, "Since you'll be sleeping in our home before we live as man and wife, I plan on carrying you across the threshold."

Delana wound her arms around his neck and looked up at him, eyes big. When he straightened up, she nodded enthusiastically, catching her lower lip in anticipation. Arthur nudged the door open for them. Dustin angled his shoulders as he stepped inside, careful not to bump his precious armful against the doorframe.

Still clasping her to his chest, he kicked the door shut, strode to the center of the cabin, and turned in a slow circle to show her the entire space. Her excitement fed into his, and he wanted to show her every inch of the place. Careful to keep her encircled in his arms, he set her on her feet.

"It's breathtaking," she marveled, still drinking in the sight of their new home.

"So are you." He waited until her eyes widened then bent to steal a kiss.

A soft sigh whispered across her lips before he felt their warm softness. He threaded his fingers through her silky blond hair, heedless of the small pins he dislodged. He savored the moment before reluctantly pulling away. His hand still twined in her lustrous curls, he smiled and gave her the product of all his hard work.

"Your home."

❧

"*Our* home," Delana corrected softly. An odd gleam flickered in Dustin's eyes before he nodded, but she attributed it to the extraordinary moment. She lightly pulled away from him to explore the house.

The Franklin stove that had stood on display at Papa's mercantile now graced the far right corner of the cabin. She ran her fingers over the iron scrollwork on the oven door.

"We'll be able to make apple pie now." She turned and smiled at him. "And apple crumb cake, too." Going back to her exploration, she admired the shelves Dustin had already installed near the stove.

"These will hold all the dry and canned goods. It was so clever of you to put them in right away." A few more steps and she stood in front of the first sparkling window. She cupped her hands as though to capture the cheery sunbeams streaming through. "I brought fabric for curtains. We'll make them up tomorrow—oh."

"It's the Lord's day," Dustin affirmed.

"Monday then." She passed the door and second window, standing in the recessed alcove beneath the loft. "It's cozy here," she praised, proud of herself for not blushing at the site where their marriage bed would soon be placed. She grasped one of the supports of the ladder leading to the loft.

"Here." Dustin took her free hand in his and curled it around the other support. He stepped back, his hands securing the ladder but his head turned as she climbed up.

"It's so roomy!" She could almost stand at her full height at the tallest point of the roofline.

"Growing room." Dustin poked his head over the top rung, but didn't join her farther in.

So our children won't be overcrowded as they grow. Delana

beamed at him as she pronounced, "It's perfect."

She climbed down the ladder, and cheers erupted as they opened the door. Soon everyone crowded in.

"I want to show you one more thing." Dustin grasped her hand and led her outside toward the small woodpile stacked against one wall. As they turned the corner, she spotted it.

"A table!" He'd chosen well-matched plank logs and sanded them to form a smooth surface atop four sturdy table legs.

"So you'll have a real kitchen." He braced both palms on the table and pressed downward to show how solidly it stood.

"Is there anything you didn't think of?" She rubbed her hand over his shoulder.

"If there is, I wouldn't know it." He grinned. "But I'm sure we'll find out about it sooner or later."

"Let's go have our last meal in the meadow," Delana invited. "We'll have supper in the house."

"Trying to bribe me into hauling everything inside?" He quirked a brow.

"Absolutely." With that, they headed toward the old cook fire one last time.

Delana's impulse was to eat as quickly as possible so they could start moving in. To her dismay, everyone else seemed ready to settle in for a well-deserved rest. She busied herself by cleaning the dishes but chafed to settle into the house.

"You seem anxious," Mama noted. "Why, when all is in readiness?"

"It's not. The men have built the house, but I've yet to do my part." Delana twisted her hands in her apron. "There's so much to do, I can't stand just sitting here!"

"Of course you cannot stand and sit at the same time."

Mama looked puzzled. "But if you want to work, we'll start and the others will join us when they're ready."

"Let's start taking some of the kitchen supplies." Delana grabbed two pans, and Mama took a sack of potatoes. Together, they tramped toward the cabin. After Delana deposited the pans on the stove and Mama set down the potatoes, they walked outside to find Dustin and Jakob bringing the table around the corner.

"Ah, the table *ist gut*." Mama nodded her approval.

"We'll need you to direct us as to where things are." Dustin backed through the door, still holding one side of the table.

"I'll consult with Cade and Isaac—they helped load the wagons." Delana took Mama's elbow, and they walked back. *Neither of us will step in a gopher hole today. Now that the cabin's ready, I'll hear no more foolish talk of sending us away.*

"We'll be unpacking, then?" Cade had already begun hitching a team of oxen to the second freight wagon. Dustin and Jakob had taken the first wagon to the cabin that morning in order to install the impossibly heavy iron stove.

"Yes." Delana peeked in the freight wagon and found it held more lumber, the saplings, and the second stove. "Wait, Cade." She walked over to the third wagon, which contained some of the furniture and linen goods. "We'll need this one today."

Soon both of the necessary wagons stood by the cabin, and Isaac unhitched the oxen and led them to pasture.

"We should unload the larger and heavier items first," Dustin reasoned. "Everything else should come later."

"The heavier items are packed farther down," Delana pointed out. "We loaded things so the wagons would be evenly weighted. The smaller items, dry goods and kitchenware, can be placed on our table or the shelves."

"Right." Dustin nodded. "Then we'll take in the larger pieces."

Gilda and Cade oversaw the unloading of the wagons while Delana and Mama went inside to shelve provisions and direct placement.

"Please lean that rug over by the stove for now." Delana pointed to the corner. The stove hadn't been lit—moving in this afternoon would make it hot enough work without the added warmth.

"We'll need nails to hang the pans and pots," Mama observed as she neatly stacked them on the table.

"Let's put the trunks atop one another, here." Delana gestured to the side of the table as clothes and linens were brought in. "Place the bolts of fabric atop them. Mama, they'll be reaching the china soon."

"I'll go see to it that they take special care." Mama bustled out of the room, and Delana could hear her through the open door and windows as she directed "Gently! These belonged to my grandmother."

Delana smiled and remembered how they'd wound heirloom quilts around the fragile pieces of glass and crystal before surrounding the china with tightly packed straw.

As men carried in pieces of the bed frame, Delana pointed them to the alcove. Dustin stomped his boots outside before coming in to attach the carved headboard and baseboard. It took three men to maneuver the surprisingly heavy feather-stuffed mattress through the door and into place. When they'd finished, the bed nestled cozily near the far corner opposite the stove.

"Please put that at the base of the bed," Delana suggested to Dustin as he and Jakob carried in her hope chest.

"The washstand goes beside the bed," Mama directed as she followed Isaac inside.

"Under the window," Delana decided as the men carried in a petite cherrywood desk. They placed her writing lap desk atop it and set a box of books beside it.

A pretty chair with turned out feet sat against the wall. She'd fetch her sewing case from the barn later.

Isaac scrambled up the ladder and positioned the bedding passed into the loft. Arthur carried in Rosalind's cradle and frowned at the ladder.

"Kaitlin will sleep in the big bed." Delana had him set the cradle nearby. Her friend couldn't climb the loft ladder with a freshly wrenched ankle, and it would be simpler to have the mother and babe on the ground floor anyway.

"Over here." Mama had Delana's wooden dish cupboard sandwiched against the wall by the kitchen window.

"That's the last of it," Delana proclaimed.

"There's a lot more." Arthur gestured toward the wagons.

"We brought furnishings and such for the other cabins as well." Gilda patted him on the shoulder. "They'll be accounted for later."

"Let's unload what's left of the lumber and consolidate the rest into one wagon." Dustin looked over both of them. "We'll dismantle the other freight wagon for more lumber. There's plenty of daylight left to begin work on the second cabin." He turned to smile at Delana: "We'll leave you women to settle in."

"Exactly." Delana nodded at him. "And we'll still have

supper ready, come the evening."

"I can hardly wait." Dustin put a hand to his stomach.

"You'll have to." She laughed and shooed him to work.

Arthur carried Kaitlin to the chair and carefully set her down. He nudged the cradle close by her before taking his leave.

"All right, ladies." Delana shut the door, and Gilda rolled up her sleeves. "We've got work to do."

thirteen

"Ahhh," Dustin exhaled a deep breath. "A good day's progress, to be followed by a fine night's meal."

"Something sure smells good—and we're still yards away from the house!" Arthur's stomach grumbled. "Not that I'd be too choosy, mind."

"What do you think they've been doing in there all afternoon?" Isaac rubbed the back of his neck as he trudged along. "We carted everything in hours ago."

"We'll find out." Dustin stopped at the shut door and gave a light knock. "Good evening, ladies!"

"One moment!" He heard the flurry of skirts come close, and he stepped back from the door to let Mrs. Albright, Gilda, and even a limping Kaitlin come out.

"Come in, Dustin!" Delana's cheerful voice brightened the already well-lit cabin.

"What's for sup—" The word died on his lips as Dustin stepped fully into the cabin and saw the full extent of what the women had done.

A blazing fire danced in the stove, warding off the chill of nearing nightfall. Woven rugs in differing shades of blue warmed the hardwood floor beside the bed and under a chair. Blue gingham curtains fell in soft folds over both windows, their color echoed in the thick quilt and feather pillows covering the bed. Fresh white towels hung over the back of the washstand, which held a cobalt blue washbasin and matching pitcher. Above the chair hung a sampler he knew must be the work of Delana's hands. In soft blue on clean white she'd stitched his favorite verse: "Faith is the substance of things hoped for, the evidence of things not seen." Everywhere he looked, he saw the thoughtful touches Delana had used to make the house he built into a welcoming home.

"What do you think?" Delana's soft voice came from beside him.

"It's true what they said." He smiled and wrapped an arm around her shoulders. "You thought of everything."

"I tried."

"The thought you've put into our home pleases me, Delana." His gaze met hers. "You made each thing my favorite color"—he cupped her cheek in his palm and clarified—"the same sweet blue as your eyes."

"Ohhh." Delana's soft sigh and flushed cheeks made him want to steal a kiss, but he realized everyone was crowded around the still-open doorway.

"If you're finished, there are some of us who've worked up an appetite." Rawhide's hopeful voice broke the tender moment as Delana laughed.

"Come in and sit down." As everyone trouped in to sit on the benches he'd made for the table, Dustin remembered how hungry he was.

"Potpie?" His mouth watered at the sight of an individual pie on every plate.

"Yes." Delana sat on the bench at the right side of one chair, waiting for him to take his place at the head of the table. Out of consideration for her sore ankle, Kaitlin sat on a stool pulled up on the far side.

Dustin took his place with a sort of humility he'd never expected. *I'm the head of this household.* The thought—and accompanying responsibility—both pleased and staggered him.

"Let's join hands and pray." Dustin held Delana's delicate hand in his right and began to thank the Lord for the blessings around him, finishing with, "And, Lord, know that there is always a place for You in the home You've seen fit to give us. Amen."

"Tomorrow's Sunday—that means we rest." Isaac shoveled a forkful of pie into his mouth.

"You deserve it." Mrs. Albright patted her youngest son's shoulder. "You've worked hard and accomplished a lot."

Now that she's lost her eldest, she dotes on her youngest son. The coddling can't continue long, or it will spoil the boy. Dustin pushed his own fork into the golden, flaky crust on his plate.

"Delicious," Arthur put Dustin's thoughts into words.

"Good company and fine food fill this house." Dustin looked around him. "There's not a thing I can think of to improve this meal."

"Perhaps a few of the raspberries I saw this afternoon." Isaac took a gulp from his cup of water.

"Oh?" Dustin had noticed Isaac's disappearance. He reasoned that the young man needed some time to grieve for the deaths in his family—away from the women.

"A little ways past the south bank of the stream," Isaac clarified. "Plump and bright red in the sunshine."

"What a wonderful find!" Delana refilled her brother's cup.

"What say we have a picnic dinner tomorrow and go berry-picking in the afternoon?" Gilda smiled at the thought. "The one who picks the most wins his or her favorite meal the next day—provided it's within reason."

"I'm in," Arthur volunteered.

"Sounds like a fun way to spend the day." Delana closed her eyes. "I do love fresh raspberries and cream.".

"We can do much with berries," Mrs. Albright added. "Come winter, we'd be glad of some preserves and such."

"I look forward to that." Dustin thought of all the tasty treats the raspberries would make possible. *Picking raspberries will be much easier than felling trees, though with no sweeter reward.* He looked at Delana, bright and animated as she chatted with the guests at their table.

"What would you do on the Lord's Day before we came?" His fiancée turned to ask him.

"Take care of the necessary things as usual, play horseshoes—"

"I'd love a rousing game of horseshoes." Isaac's smile faded as Dustin gave him a stern look over his interruption.

"I see no reason why that can't be part of our picnic!" Delana rubbed her hands together. "Maybe I'll try it, too. I like a challenge. I've heard that the most difficult things can be the most rewarding."

Dustin snapped his gaze from Arthur to Delana. *That's the same thing Arthur said to me when we spoke of sending the women home. But what could the significance be?* Her sweet smile revealed nothing. *Ridiculous to think there's a connection. It was good advice then, and it's doubtless been given many times.* "Then we'll do it together," he told her.

"I'd be grateful for your guidance and expertise." Her eyes sparkled. "Though I might damage your standing."

Dustin couldn't resist boasting, "My reputation can handle it."

"Listen to him speak as though he's the champion," Jakob scoffed. "A happy throw every now and again doesn't tell of perfected technique."

"It tells of skill," Dustin rebutted.

"If it's skill that tells the measure of the man," Arthur enjoined, "then you'll soon see me standing tall."

"You're unparalleled at throws so far they seem impossible, but you overshoot those nearer to the mark. We take one step back after each throw to make the competition more interesting," Dustin explained their unusual rule to Delana.

" 'Tis always better to surpass the mark than fall short of it." Arthur winked at his wife. "So I'll take that as a compliment."

"And I'll take it as my first lesson." Delana smiled up at Dustin. "I look forward to many more."

≈

After a morning devotion led by Cade, Delana began preparing a picnic dinner.

Kaitlin sat with her at the table as they set to plucking four of the scarce supply of chickens they'd brought for eating. They carefully stowed the feathers in a sack between them to stuff a mattress later.

"Fried chicken and biscuits will put smiles on their faces." Gilda crumbled leftover bread into fine crumbs.

They dressed, cleaned, and cut the chickens into pieces before sizzles sounded in the kitchen.

"The men are with the horseshoes." Mama packed the biscuits, butter, and preserves into a basket. "Practicing."

"It should be a day to remember." Gilda set another piece of crispy chicken on the platter.

"I hope so." Delana set out a few of the blankets the men

wore out over the past year. "The weather's lovely, and everyone is in good spirits since the house is up."

"A good night's sleep didn't hurt." Kaitlin chuckled. "The house is an improvement for us, but the men like the tack room in the barn far better than the bare earth."

Delana stacked buckets for raspberry picking. "It was so clever of Dustin, Jakob, and Arthur to clear the area where the three claims meet."

"Mmmmhmmm." Kaitlin picked up Rosalind, who'd begun to fuss. "The cleared land provides perfect places for our cabins, so we're close as can be."

"And our claim will follow." Gilda covered the full platter with a cloth and set about filling the next one.

"Ist gut to have friends for neighbors." Mama smiled at Gilda and Kaitlin.

" 'Twill be just as good to have neighbors for friends." Kaitlin smiled back.

When the chicken was crispy, the dishes washed, and everything packed for the picnic, they called the men and set off. Delana spread the old blankets under the shade of a grove of trees. From where they sat, everyone could see tantalizing red glimpses of the wild raspberries hanging in their brambly bushes.

"I love fried chicken." Isaac brandished a drumstick and set to with enthusiasm.

"I know." Mama passed him a biscuit.

"You know, I'd thought to ask for fried chicken after I win the raspberry-picking contest." Jakob took a bite and chewed thoughtfully. "Time to start thinking of something else."

"Let me know what you come up with," Rawhide directed.

"I'll take it into consideration when *I* win that contest."

"No matter who picks the most berries," Dustin remarked, "every one of us will win a delicious dinner so long as these women are working the stove."

Was it just three days ago I told him I wasn't sure he liked my cooking? How strange it is that it seems like we've been here so much longer than six days, yet the time doesn't drag on. We pack so much into every day out here that we experience more to remember. Pleased with the thought, Delana stood up. "Who's ready to stop planning their win and start picking those berries?"

"I'll stay here." Kaitlin cuddled a now drowsy Rosalind. "It's best not to wake her, and my ankle isna ready for me to go gallivantin' around yet. But pick plenty for me!"

"We will," Dustin promised her as he grabbed Delana's hand and gently pulled her toward the grouping of raspberry bushes. Isaac saw them edging over and loped past them.

"The race is on." Delana looked at their entwined hands, loathe to let go. Still. . . "I'm going to need my hand if I'm to have any chance!"

"Just remember," Dustin stopped speaking as he raised her hand to his lips for a kiss that sent shivers down her spine. "This hand belongs to me and will soon wear my ring."

She squeezed his hand. "I never forgot."

fourteen

Dustin cast a furtive glance toward Delana's fourth bucket then at his own, which was only his third. Happily, he'd perfected a way of evening the odds and had been employing it for the past half hour or so. He couldn't have gotten away with it if they could simply fill the buckets with berries. Their harvest was too fragile—the bottom berries would be crushed if they put more than a few layers in the bucket.

He waited until she straightened up to take a few steps away from the already-plucked area she'd harvested. He pounced. Snitching another plump red berry from the top of her bucket, he bit into the sweet fruit.

"What are you up to?" Alerted by his sudden movements, Delana turned and narrowed her eyes.

"Picking raspberries," he said blithely. Dustin stooped to add more of them to his own stash—and to hide his grin. This wouldn't be nearly as much fun without her, so he wasn't about to have Delana finish before him. *I wonder how many times I can do that before she notices that her pail should be much heavier.* He bent to gather another handful and had more difficulty than when he'd started. *More importantly, how many raspberries can I eat before I pop?*

"Do you remember the woman who obeyed the prophet Elijah? She poured out her small supply of oil, only to find that, though it should be gone, her jar didn't empty no matter how many times she poured out the oil?" Delana gestured toward her pail. "I think this bucket is the opposite of that. No matter how many berries I put inside, it never becomes full."

"Oh?" Dustin struggled not to laugh at her disgruntled expression.

"Although," she mused, glancing at her pail as she added another handful of raspberries, "it doesn't even feel heavier."

"Maybe we could work something out." Dustin moved his pail closer to hers. "If we move some of your berries into my bucket, it would have as many berries as it could hold without crushing them. Then I could carry yours while we fill it." *Even better, you'll stand closer to me.*

"It looks about equal," she decided after scrutinizing his crop. She began transferring some of hers to round out his pail. "There." Delana handed him her lightened load.

He edged closer as they redoubled their efforts. With their teamwork—and the bonus of him not sneaking a raspberry every time her back was turned—their pail filled rapidly.

"We work well together." Dustin lifted their harvest for her inspection, stepping so close he imagined he caught a whiff of lilacs from her.

Delana tried to stand but toppled from the unexpected burden of Dustin's boots on her pooled skirts. "You're stepping on my dress!" As she lost her balance, his arm shot out and snaked around her waist.

"Gotcha." With her pressed to his side, Dustin wanted to taste her sweet lips in the afternoon sunshine. He contented himself with offering her a raspberry. "I'd say we deserve a little reward."

"Mmmm." She savored the luscious fruit before selecting

another. "Here's one for you—if you've any room left in your stomach."

"I did put away a lot of that fried chicken," Dustin agreed before accepting the proffered fruit.

"Ah." Delana raised a brow. "I thought you might be full from all the raspberries you've sneaked."

Dustin stopped chewing and gaped at her. "You knew?"

"Of course I knew." She giggled. "I thought it was funny, how you'd look so pleased with yourself every time I turned back around."

"What gave me away?" He set down the pail.

"The juice on your chin." She reached up to brush it away with her fingertips.

Dustin held his breath at the softness of her touch. *Lord, this day of rest has made me anxious to finish my work. The second cabin must be built before the circuit preacher comes.* Delana put her hand on his forearm, bracing herself as she lifted their harvest.

And, Lord? Please let the preacher come soon!

&

Delana rubbed her thumb across fingertips still tingling from their brush with Dustin's slightly stubbled chin. He'd made her want to giggle as he boyishly filched her raspberries, but the slightest touch reminded her he was all man.

"Arthur beat us," she noted as they left the wild patch.

"No matter." Dustin waved the loss away. "He's pounding the stake for horseshoes. Now the fun really begins."

"Hmmph." Delana pretended to be affronted. "So berry-picking with me wasn't fun?"

"Oh, I enjoyed it," he assured her, "but it's the prospect of teaching you to play that I'm looking forward to."

"So am I, but Mama disapproves. She says horseshoes are for men."

"The game is played by men," Dustin agreed. "Still, what reason is there not to let a woman try? It's not a dangerous sport."

"So you would agree that I shouldn't participate were it more dangerous?" Delana gave him a sideways glance. "Women are capable of more than some men think." She waited for his answer, wondering if he sensed its import.

"I never underestimate a woman." He caught her free hand in his and squeezed gently. "You've proven you're a force to be reckoned with."

Thank You, Lord! He sees that I am strong enough to live and work alongside him. The house was a turning point in his way of thinking, I believe. Now we're a team, the way it should always be.

"We're both stronger when we work together." She squeezed back.

"I'll catch the rabbits, and you'll cook them." Dustin smiled, but said no more.

"You muck the stables, and I'll milk the cows." She needed him to see that their partnership extended beyond one simple instance.

"I'll clear the land and turn the soil, while you plant the garden," he caught on.

"I'll make preserves out of the raspberries we picked together." She set the pail down by Arthur's.

"Yes." Dustin set his beside hers. "I've built the oven where you'll bake the bread."

"You wear through your socks, and I'll darn them." Delana

frowned. "Actually, that doesn't seem quite even."

"I'll find a way to make it up to you." The gleam in his eye made Delana move a step closer.

"Come on, you two!" Isaac set down his half-filled bucket and hurried toward Arthur, who checked to see that the stake held fast.

The closeness of the moment shattered, Delana strove to recapture the lightheartedness they shared by the berries. "How about *I* find the way, and you still make it up to me." She tapped her index finger to her chin. "It bears thinking on—we've already darned and stitched a pile of your clothes."

"That sounds ominous." Dustin led her over to the cleared area where they'd play the game. "Maybe I'll have to keep you distracted."

"Good idea," she teased. "You can start by teaching me to toss this." Delana casually leaned over to pluck a horseshoe from the grass and moved around to find the best pitching spot.

"Steady, now." Dustin's warm hands curled around her shoulders, giving her support. "Move it from hand to hand to get a feel for its balance before you toss it."

Delana transferred the piece of curved iron from one hand to the other, testing its heft. "Is there a way you hold it when you toss?"

"Yes, though different people do so differently." His hands moved down her arms to cover her own. He adjusted the way she held the horseshoe. "You draw your arm back, like so." He carried her through the motion as he instructed. "Sight your target and judge the distance, and then tense to give it all your strength and control."

Delana tried to control the wild galloping of her heart, all too aware of his broad chest at her back, his strong arm guiding hers. *I've never felt so safe and so jumpy at the same time.*

When he took his hand away, the horseshoe slipped through her suddenly nerveless fingers to the ground. The warm spring day felt unexpectedly cool as he stepped away to retrieve it.

"If it were possible to use both hands, I'd have you try that since you're so dainty." Dustin frowned in thought. "But you don't get the same range or accuracy."

"Let me try with one hand a couple of times." Delana tried to ignore the way Arthur, Rawhide, and Isaac quickly distanced themselves from both her and the stake. She pulled the horseshoe up and flung it toward the stake. Or rather, she meant to throw it toward the stake. It landed embarrassingly wide—and short of the post.

"This time," Dustin suggested as he handed her the next one, "try it with your eyes open so you can aim."

She tried again but gained nothing save a rapidly tiring wrist. Disgruntled, she turned to Dustin. "You said something about using both hands?"

"Yes, but you'll recall I mentioned it worsened aim." Dustin gave her an infuriating grin. "To tell the truth, you can't afford to lose any ground."

"She can't get any worse." Rawhide blew a sour note on a blade of grass. "Let her give it one more try, then the real contenders can start the competition."

"Give it everything, liebling," Mama rooted for her, throwing Rawhide a dirty glance. "Show them what the Albright women can do!"

"Right!" Delana, surprised that her mother suddenly seemed to support her horseshoe endeavor, put on a good outward show, but inwardly groaned. *Mama really shouldn't have made the Albright pride rest on this. Lord, I know it's too much to ask that I ring this horseshoe around the post. All the same, I'd ask You to guide my hand so that it comes closer this time!*

Abandoning all pretense at good form, Delana clutched the horseshoe in both hands, braced her feet shoulder width apart, and gave a mighty underhand heave as she shut her eyes.

Clang! The blessed sound made her open her eyes. The men gaped at her accomplishment.

"Yes!" She tugged on Dustin's sleeve. "Did you *see?*"

"You hit the post and glanced off," Dustin marveled. "Who would've thought. . ."

Mama put her hands on her hips. "I did. *Mein* liebling can do anything she minds."

"You mean anything she puts her mind to, Mama." Jakob grinned.

"Ja." Mama agreed before shaking a finger at her son. "But you mind your Mama."

"Are you going to compete?" Isaac asked Delana.

"I've had enough for today." She started walking toward Kaitlin. "After all, it's better to surpass the mark than fall short of it."

fifteen

With a feminine audience on hand, the men competed more fiercely than usual. Dustin, determined not to be outdone by Delana's throw, took his sweet time eyeing the distance.

"It ain't movin', and the women are the other way," Rawhide burst out after a while. "No reason to stare that long."

Dustin ignored both the scout and the giggles coming from the shade. With a deep breath and a quick prayer, he launched the horseshoe toward the post.

The resounding *clang* and subsequent whirring as the horseshoe spiraled down the post brought a triumphant smile to his lips. "Now there's a reason to stare."

Walking with a bit of a self-satisfied swagger, Dustin helped himself to a dipperful of cool water as Isaac tried his hand. The youngster's toss listed too far left, and he threw his hat to the ground in disgust.

The late afternoon whirled by in a flurry of *whooshes* followed by satisfying *clangs* or disheartening *thumps* as the horseshoe hit the ground. Dustin earned most of the former, earning him a smile from Delana and scowls from the other men.

"I knew you would win." Delana's confidence made him walk a bit taller.

"I'm sorry to see the sun setting." Isaac's lament made Dustin realize how quickly the day had gone by.

"We have a lot to do tomorrow," Dustin agreed. "The second

cabin will go up faster than the first."

"It only took you five days to build ours." Delana's brow furrowed. "That's already so speedy!"

"True." Arthur gazed into the distance where his cabin would be the next structure on the horizon. " 'Tis simply we'll be more skilled at the work. Then, too, we built your summer oven in that time."

"I'll cherish the day." Kaitlin's soft smile bespoke a woman looking forward to settling in her own home.

The women gathered the blankets while the men toted the pails of berries. The night's chill would keep them fresh without the benefit of a springhouse.

After a substantial supper of biscuits and gravy, the men trooped off to catch some sleep. Dustin reached the tack room just before the others. Still basking in the contentment of the day, he set his lantern on an upturned crate.

"I can't believe she hit that post." He kicked his boots off and prepared to go to bed. The straw-filled sack mattress seemed soft as fluffy white clouds after sleeping on the unforgiving ground. Dustin hoped the extra blankets he'd left with the freight drivers would help make them more comfortable.

"Lucky shot," Isaac grunted. "My sister was smart to stop when she did."

"On second thought," Dustin mused, "I believe it. My Delana has spirit and determination." He settled back and added, "Not to mention a good teacher."

"Her toss had nothin' to do wi' your teachin'." Cade shook his head. "I never heard you tell her to grab the thing and heft it blindly, with both eyes closed."

"I was right by her. She aimed before she closed her eyes."

Dustin set the record straight.

"Call it what you will." Rawhide pulled up his blanket. "The thing I can't believe is that Arthur picked the most raspberries."

Recalling the prize, they all turned to stare at the victor, who nonchalantly pretended he didn't notice the attention.

"What did you choose?" Jakob looked suspiciously at Arthur, who was whistling. "It wasn't that sheep's stomach thing you were telling us about before, was it?"

"He wouldn't do that to us," Dustin broke in. He looked at Arthur's cat-with-the-canary grin and thought twice. "Would you?"

"I dearly love my haggis," Arthur drew out his response, "and well my Kaitlin knows it." He plumped his pillow and turned over without saying another word.

"Oh no, you don't." Dustin aimed his own pillow at the blacksmith's head. "We don't have any sheep, so that couldn't be it even if you were that ornery."

"You should try haggis before you judge it." Cade sounded aggrieved. " 'Tis a traditional Scottish dish."

"I'll make you a deal," Jakob yawned. "You don't make me try it, and I won't judge it."

"Pah." Cade rolled his eyes. " 'Tis good for the likes of you. Puts hair on your chest."

"Douse the lantern and quit yammerin'," Rawhide grumbled.

"I'll second that," Arthur yawned.

"You'll get no sleep until I've got peace of mind." Isaac nudged Arthur with his elbow. "I'm not trying any mystery dish."

"This much I'll be tellin' ye, and no more." Arthur sat up

and glowered at the lot of them, his burr thick with fatigue. "I chose Kaitlin's favorite dish as she couldna pick the berries wi' her sore ankle."

"Ah." Cade nodded and drew his blanket over his shoulders.

"What's Kaitlin's favorite?" Isaac and Jakob turned to Cade and voiced the question as one.

"I'll be honorin' Arthur's choice." Cade stretched and smiled. "Though I will say that my daughter's as true a Scot as her husband."

Dustin, Jakob, and Isaac groaned loudly.

"Hush up," Rawhide groused at them. "Whatever it is, it will fill your bellies when they're empty. Even the women will have quit running their mouths and turned in by now. Let's get some shut eye." With that, he snuffed the light, plunging the tack room into darkness.

"Men, Cade's going to tell us his daughter's favorite dish before he falls asleep," Dustin stated cheerfully. "Because he has only one other option."

"Oh?" Cade challenged.

"Yep." Dustin didn't bother to smother his chuckle. "Otherwise I'll tell Gilda what you said when you first got here."

"What did I say?"

"That you didn't think you could have made it one more day, traveling with a passel of women," Dustin reminded him gleefully. Silence stretched so long he began to wonder if the older man had fallen asleep.

"Cinnamon buns." Cade's quiet answer brought a smile to Dustin's lips.

Cinnamon buns, Dustin thought as his eyes drifted shut and rest claimed him. *I can almost smell the. . .*

❧

Scents of cinnamon and sweet icing in the kitchen made Delana think of Christmas. One of her earliest memories was of Mama making the dough for *apfel borogie*, a special pastry she served every Christmas morning. She rolled it flat, filled it with apples seasoned by cinnamon and nutmeg, and then braided the outer strips of dough into a soft woven strudel.

The recipe matched the dough for cinnamon buns. Mama made extra and slathered it with butter, sugar, and cinnamon before rolling it into a spiral. Then she sliced the rolls and baked them. Though she never told Mama, Delana always chose her cinnamon bun before they even made it to the oven. Without fail, Hans would swipe that exact bun from the platter before Delana even finished icing them.

Her girlish memory took on the pain of loss. *I'll never bake him another cinnamon roll. Hans will never spend Christmas with us again.* The fragrance filling the kitchen filled her with grief as well. Cinnamon memories of Hans had her blinking back unexpected tears.

"Hans?" Mama, who shared those same memories, had obviously recognized the sheen of tears in Delana's eyes and came to wrap her in a warm hug.

"I miss him," Delana sniffled. "Papa died before I could understand that Hans will never come home." *And I wouldn't let myself think of it even then. The effort to keep everyone together and get us here took all I had.*

"It is right that we miss them." Mama's clasp tightened. "God's children are missed long after He takes them home. Hans and your Papa are with the Lord—it is hard for us, the ones who stay behind."

"Yes." Delana pulled away and patted her hair back into place. "But we have Jakob and Isaac to think of now."

"And Dustin." Mama smiled softly. "Isaac says nothing of joining the war since we came here."

"I know." Delana drew a relieved breath. Isaac's determination to avenge his brother's death had caused her and Mama many sleepless nights during the journey. She thanked the Lord once again for Cade, whose keen eye and tactful maintenance had ensured that Isaac didn't attempt the foolish venture.

"There is empty place in the heart," Mama commiserated. "But we fill the days and God loves us through them."

"You're wise, Mama." Delana gave a slight smile. *Thank You, Lord, for bringing her so far from the grief-stricken woman who wouldn't speak for three days after news of Hans's death, and mourned so deeply she couldn't sleep after her husband's passing. Now, Mama comforts me. You've given her strength when I could no longer carry us both in grief.*

She planted a kiss atop Mama's dark blond hair, now threaded liberally with white. "We'd best get this batch in the oven. Kaitlin and Gilda will be back with the cream from last night's milking any moment."

"Ja." Mama took the pan while Delana wiped the tabletop with a kitchen rag.

"Here's the cream." Kaitlin entered the cabin with a slight limp, her mother right behind her.

"I've sliced some of the raspberries and added a bit of sugar for sweetness." Delana placed the large bowl beside Kaitlin, who added cream. Its cool whiteness took on a pink tinge from the juicy berries as she stirred gently.

With that done, Delana got up to pour milk into the tin

cups, leaving Kaitlin to sit and drizzle icing on the finished buns.

"It's so sweet that Arthur chose your favorite," Delana told her friend.

"Yes, though he might not deserve so much credit." Kaitlin took on an almost impish air. "They're one of his favorite treats, too."

"He's very clever." Gilda bustled over with the last tray, sliding it far enough away that Kaitlin wouldn't burn herself on the still-hot edge.

"Talking about me when I'm not around?" Rawhide stuck his head through the door. "And you say I need manners."

"Ja, you do." Mama motioned for him to come inside. "Thinking you're the only clever man here—such arrogance!"

"Ha!" Rawhide waggled his brows. "So you do think I'm a clever man."

"I think you're more a difficult one."

"No, just hungry." Rawhide swiped a finger full of icing from the bowl she carried past and received a whack on the back of his hand for his efforts. He jerked away in surprise before grumbling, "No one can tell me that was ladylike."

Delana smiled as she watched them bicker. Rawhide's needling brought out Mama's strong will. Whether the ornery man knew it or not, he'd helped Mama in the midst of deepest grief.

The men shouldered into the cabin, eagerly sniffing the fragrant air around them. After the blessing, it seemed Delana had hardly taken three bites before all the cinnamon rolls vanished from the table. *Even after we made two extra batches!* The berries and cream didn't last much longer, but the men were all smiles as they set back to work.

"I've never seen food disappear so quickly!" Gilda *tsk-tsk*ed as she piled dirty dishes.

"Here." Delana pressed a cinnamon bun, the one without icing, into Kaitlin's hand. "I saved one for Arthur—a reward for his good choice."

"Thankee." Kaitlin wrapped it in a cloth napkin and tucked it in one of her apron pockets. "I'm sure he'll enjoy that."

They finished tidying up after the morning meal and turned their attention to the surfeit of berries they'd gathered. Even after this morning's meal and yesterday's playful tasting, they had a generous supply.

Gilda began boiling a load of them down, adding a little sugar. When the mixture was thick, they'd spread it on sheets of paper to dry before rolling the preserves for storage.

"Let me get these out of the way." Delana took the raspberries she'd combined with white vinegar and placed the bowl at the other end of the table. Adding some of this sweet syrup mixture to a pitcher of water made a refreshing drink, almost like lemonade, only with raspberries. "I know it takes a couple of days to make it, but I love raspberry quencher."

"I hope it turns out well." Kaitlin tucked Rosalind into the cradle and limped back to the table.

All four women sat around the table, paring knives in hand, and began to halve a large pile of raspberries. Slowly, the sliced berries, layered generously with sugar, filled one of their largest stewpots. By the time they'd finished, Delana's entire hands were stained red. She covered the berries and sugar, pushing the pot over by the raspberry quencher mixture.

"We'll boil that and make jam after dinner." Gilda checked

on the mixture boiling at the stove. "This is ready to spread and dry."

"The fruit leathers will be useful during winter." Mama placed paper on the table. "When boiled, they're as wonderful in pies and such as when they were fresh. Some say even better."

"Hard to imagine." Delana popped a raspberry into her mouth and savored its tart sweetness.

"Someday you'll see for yourself." Mama gave her a knowing smile. "Most things get better with age."

sixteen

Four days later, Dustin waited outside the second cabin as Arthur gave Kaitlin the tour of their own home. This cabin was built as the mirror image of Dustin and Delana's, with a stone fireplace taking up most of one wall instead of a stove.

Something moved on the horizon, capturing his attention. Dustin squinted but could only make out a lone rider approaching at a steady pace. Normally, he'd assume it was Rawhide, but his friend stood beside him. Dustin strode toward the approaching figure. "Parson Booker."

"Looks as though you've been keeping busy," the visitor observed as he dismounted.

"We have indeed, and so have you. It's been too long since you came." Dustin grinned. "What news from the civilized world?"

"Last week this was officially declared the Montana Territory." Preacher Booker clapped him on the back. "The first step toward statehood."

"Good news, indeed! And I've some news of my own to celebrate." Dustin grasped the reins of the parson's mare and walked her over to where everyone began streaming out of the cabin. "My bride-to-be arrived a little less than two weeks ago."

"Looks like she brought a few friends." Parson Booker raised his eyebrows at the gathering crowd.

"I'll take his horse to the barn." Rawhide led her away,

freeing Dustin to draw Delana forward.

"Preacher Booker, this is Miss Delana Albright, my fiancée." Dustin went on to introduce Mrs. Albright, Isaac, and the Bannings. Arthur presented Kaitlin and Rosalind.

"Nice to meet all of you." Though the preacher smiled, he seemed uneasy. "Had I known the population increased so, I would have come sooner."

"You're welcome here anytime," Dustin assured him. "We're glad to see you."

"I ran late in Virginia City." The preacher's brown eyes filled with regret. "A mining rights disagreement—I stayed to see three men buried."

"I'm sorry to hear that." Dustin removed his hat, and the other men followed suit for a moment of silence.

"How long you will stay?" Mrs. Albright glanced at Delana and Dustin. "We have much to plan."

"I'm to officiate at my sister's wedding in Charleston." The preacher gave a heavy sigh. "I catch a steamboat at Fort Benton in three days."

"But Fort Benton is three days away!" Delana burst out. "You will miss your sister's wedding unless you leave tomorrow morning."

"Yes." Preacher Booker looked at Dustin. "Is there any reason why the wedding should not take place today? I've no notion when I might return. It could be months, and I'd like to see you two settled in God's sight before I leave."

"Excuse us." Dustin ushered a speechless Delana into the new cabin for a moment of privacy. He braced her with a hand on either shoulder.

"Today?" When she found her voice, it emerged in a squeak.

"Today." He answered the question firmly. "We've waited for one another an entire year, Delana." He tilted her chin, meeting her troubled gaze. "Your father asked you to bring the family here to provide you the support a husband can supply. The security *I* will give you."

"I know." Delana nibbled on her lower lip. "I had thought to have more time. . ."

"We've a life full of sweet moments before us." He cupped her cheek with his palm. "I'm anxious to begin it."

"Oh, Dustin." Her bright blue eyes swam with tears. "I'll not keep you waiting. I'd always thought my father would walk me down the aisle. I'd meet you in a pure white dress and veil, carrying a bouquet of flowers. Now there'll be no aisle, nor a wedding gown, but those don't matter. I just wish Papa was here."

"He wished this for us." Dustin gathered her in the circle of his arms as she shed a few tears. When she leaned back and offered a watery smile, he knew she was ready. "Let your unbound hair be your veil, and put on the blue dress that matches your eyes. You'll wear all the promise of the beautiful Montana sky as we wed."

"I'd like that. It speaks of limitless possibility." Delana nodded. "What could be more fitting?" She smoothed her skirts while he opened the door.

"Come, come." Mrs. Albright ushered Delana toward their cabin, followed closely by Kaitlin and Gilda.

As soon as the door closed behind them, Dustin sprang into action.

"Arthur!" Dustin angled one of his friend's benches out the door. "Would you grab the other?" He took his bench to

an old bur oak just yards away from the cabin he'd built for
Delana. He set it down beneath the high arcs of the branches,
and Arthur followed suit.

"What else can we do?" The blacksmith looked around for
inspiration.

"Actually," Dustin was seized with sudden inspiration.
"There is one thing. . ."

&

Delana winced as Mama ruthlessly twisted her hair into a
too-tight upswept knot. "Dustin asked me to wear it down."
She gratefully pulled away from the brush her mother wielded
like a bristly weapon.

"I will put your lilac oil in the wash water." Mama hurried
away.

"Here." Kaitlin pressed something into her hand. "I wore
it on my wedding day. 'Twould honor me if you'd use it on
yours."

Delana stopped running the brush through her golden
curls to look at the hairclip resting in her palm. An intricately
looped design, delicately worked in silver, caught the faint
light coming through the windows. "It's beautiful." She
reached out to hug her friend.

A knock sounded on the door. Delana's heart thudded. *It's
been only a few moments. I'm not ready yet!*

"The groom asked me to deliver summat." Arthur's words
galvanized Delana to stand before her mirror. She caught
a few locks in the lovely clip, leaving the rest of her hair to
tumble down her back. Her head felt oddly light.

"Dustin wanted you to have these." Arthur held out a small
posy of wild blue hyacinth. "He said his bride would have a

bouquet to match her dress."

"Oh." Tears welled into her eyes as she held her bridal bouquet. *Dustin did his best to make this the wedding of my dreams.* The delicate flowers she held were worth more than any amount of gold. *This is a symbol of his love.*

When Arthur left, Delana slid out of her work dress and cleansed herself with the cool, lilac-scented water. She slipped into her blue dress and looked around at the home Dustin had built for her.

When next I step into the house, I'll be a wife. Delana took a deep breath. *Lord, the time is short, so I'll be brief. Thank You for Dustin, and please help me be a good wife to him. Be with us this day and throughout our marriage. Amen.*

"I'm ready." She smoothed her skirts one last time, took the bouquet from her mother's hands, and stepped outside.

Jakob waited outside the door, tucking her hand into the crook of his arm. "You look beautiful, Ana. Papa would be proud."

Delana blinked back tears at the sweet words. *Papa would be proud that we are all here, together. If only he could be here to share this moment with us.*

Everyone waited under the bur oak tree, seated on the benches but looking over their shoulders to watch her progress. Isaac sat beside Mama, Gilda with Cade, and Kaitlin with Arthur, who held Rosalind in the crook of one arm. Rawhide and the freight drivers filled the other bench.

Delana knew they were all smiling, sharing her joy, but she had eyes only for Dustin. He stood straight and tall in his Sunday best, his gaze fixed upon her. Jakob led her toward Preacher Booker.

"Who gives this woman to be wed?" The preacher asked, his voice rich and solemn.

"I do." Jakob grasped her hand, guiding her to Dustin's arm.

Delana clutched her hyacinth bouquet as her brother gave her away. She smiled into Dustin's hazel eyes. " 'I am my beloved's, and my beloved is mine.' I'm ready now."

≈

Dustin stood before Preacher Booker, watching Jakob walk Delana toward him. He drank in the sight of his bride, radiant in the soft blue with her golden curls cascading around her sweet face. She held a small bouquet of the blue wildflowers he'd picked as she came to him.

After this day, Delana will be my wife forever. The thought overwhelmed him as Jakob placed her small hand on his arm, symbolically giving her over to Dustin's care.

" 'I am my beloved's, and my beloved is mine,' " he repeated to her before turning to the parson. *Mine.* Preacher Booker's words seemed to be coming from a far distance, but somehow Dustin echoed the proper vows at the right time.

Just as the sun set, the preacher pronounced them man and wife. Dustin gathered Delana in his arms and silently promised to begin this marriage the right way. All coherent thought fled as he kissed his bride. When he reluctantly let her go, he blurted out the first thing that came to his mind. In the flickering light from the lanterns, he asked his beloved, "Are you hungry?"

"What?" Delana sounded surprised. "Not right now—oh!" Her answer faded to a gasp when Dustin scooped her into his arms.

"Good." Amid the cheers of their family and friends, he

carried his prize to their home. For the second time, he carried her over the threshold.

Delana kept her arms circled around his neck, her head nestled against his chest. "Dustin?"

"Yes?" He gently kicked the door shut and stood there in the dark, waiting to hear what she had to tell him.

"I love you."

"I love you, too." He carefully set her on her feet and held her close. "The wedding might not have been what you imagined, Delana"—he paused to kiss her softly before adding—"but I promise you this: our marriage will be all you hoped for."

seventeen

Two months as a married woman had agreed with Delana. That, along with the secret knowledge she held in her heart, made the prospect of Independence Day bearable.

Tomorrow will mark one year since Hans fell at the Battle of Vicksburg, and still this terrible war rages on. The anniversary of his death will be a difficult remembrance, but my joyous news will help keep Mama from sinking into her grief. Delana pressed her hands against her still-trim tummy and smiled.

Lord, thank You for the many blessings You've given me. On the same night Dustin and I began our life together, You created the precious life growing inside me. Please keep my baby safe and let the child give Mama a reason to rejoice tomorrow on a day of mingled sorrow and freedom.

With a full heart, she moved down the garden row she was weeding. *I've said nothing even to Dustin of my hopes, unsure until so recently that I carried our child. Tonight, when it's just the two of us in our home, he'll hear the news first.* Delana finished pulling the weeds from her section and went to fetch a dipper of water. The cool liquid refreshed her.

"Nein! Oh, nein." Mama's anguished cry had Delana running toward the henhouse.

"Mama?" She skidded to a stop next to her tear-streaked mother.

"Isaac!" Mama clutched a piece of paper filled with the spiky

134

writing of her youngest son. She thrust it toward Delana, her face ashen as she repeated, "Isaac!"

Delana put one arm around her stunned parent and scanned the hastily written note:

Mama,

I have gone to fight the confederates who took Hans's life. You and Jakob have a cabin now, and Delana and Dustin are married and settled. You don't need me to help take care of you, so I go to help win this war for Hans.

Love,
Isaac

She dimly heard the rush of footsteps behind her before the roaring in her ears took away all sense of sound, and the blackness closed in.

❧

Delana awoke to find herself lying on the bed she shared with Dustin, who stood beside her.

"Are you all right?" He squatted to be at eye level and smoothed a hand over her hair.

"I think so." Delana's hands went to her stomach. "Oh, Isaac." Tears stung her eyes.

"Jakob and I will search for him." Dustin straightened up. "With God's guidance, I'll bring him home."

"Thank you." Mama stood at the foot of the bed, wringing her hands. Her gaze fixed upon Delana, she didn't speak again until Jakob and Dustin headed to the barn.

"How far along?" Mama's soft question had Delana hugging her middle.

"Two months." She closed her eyes, dismayed to find her joyous news become another concern.

"We already loosened your stays." Gilda shook her head. " 'Tis not good for the babe, you being cinched in."

"Promise me," Delana croaked out the words, "you won't tell Dustin."

" 'Tis not our news to tell." Kaitlin's brow wrinkled. "Though it willna be kept hidden for long."

"I know." Delana looked at the three women around her. "It only needs to wait until Jakob and Dustin bring Isaac home."

If Dustin knew I carried his babe, he wouldn't leave me. Right now, the most important thing is that he finds my brother and brings him home. Oh, Isaac. . .

❧

When he found the boy, he would hog-tie him and sling him over the saddle so the kid couldn't run off again.

Dustin's jaw clenched. How could Isaac do this to Delana and their mother? Four fruitless days of searching hadn't brought a satisfactory answer. With Jakob headed in the opposite direction, Dustin had only his own rage for company.

Lord, Delana has already lost one brother and her father in such a short period of time. I understand Isaac's grief over Hans's death, but a headstrong fifteen-year-old will be in his grave before he witnesses justice. All Isaac can accomplish by this foolish plan is breaking the hearts of his mother and sister. Please let me find him, Lord. I can't bear the thought of going home empty-handed.

Sleep claimed him for the night after he finished his prayer. Despite exhaustion from four days of hard riding, memories of Delana's tear-filled eyes plagued him through the night.

He awoke feeling no more rested than when he'd made

camp. Dustin tried to pin down a course of action.

He'd traveled due east in case Isaac had been fool enough to try crossing the wilderness on horseback. The boy would run out of provisions—if he were lucky and had no other troubles.

I rode hard. Either Isaac pressed on, keeping a frantic pace to stay ahead of me, or he didn't come this way. I pray Jakob overtook his brother on the way to Fort Benton. He reached for the saddlebags he'd left lying next to him. If he chased after Isaac even one more day, Dustin wouldn't have the supplies to return home himself. *I'll return home with nothing to show for the days lost.* Stomach growling, Dustin rummaged in one of his saddlebags.

His fingers closed around a bag of beans, but the back of his hand brushed against something warm and. . .furry? Dustin snatched his hand out of the bag. *Raccoon. Lucky thing this one's still sleeping. It would've clawed my hand and arm to bits were it awake.* Dustin stood up, stepped back, and shook the contents of the bag onto the ground. Out tumbled coffee, a fork and pie tin, a few bags of beans, some jerky, and a small gray. . .kitten?

Awakened so rudely, the tiny cat opened its mouth and made a piteous mewling sound. The furry bundle crouched low to the ground, light green eyes looking at Dustin hopefully.

"What are you doing out here, cat?" Dustin hadn't come across anyone for four days. He gently scooped the little scamp into his hands and looked it over. "You're no wildcat."

In response, the kitten rubbed its head against his fingers. When Dustin stroked the softness of its fur, the little cat's chest rumbled with a raspy purr.

In that instant, Dustin knew he wouldn't be coming home as

empty-handed as he'd thought. There'd be a furry addition to his and Delana's home. He found the thought oddly soothing.

I may not be able to bring her brother home safe and sound, but she'll have something cuddly to comfort her a tiny bit.

"Let's make some breakfast." He held his new friend in one hand and reached for some jerky with the other. "Now, what am I going to name you?"

&

Delana stepped away from the heat of the boiling wash kettle, bearing a shirt on the long paddle. She tipped it into the bucket of rinse water and closed her eyes.

It's so hot. She placed the tip of the paddle on the ground and used it to brace herself as she mopped her forehead. Although she'd not kept down the few bites of toast she'd managed to swallow that day, her stomach churned.

She stretched, turning slightly to ease the kink in her lower back before rejoining the others at the stream. She saw something from the corner of her eye and snapped to attention.

Shading her eyes, she squinted and could just make out the figures of men approaching on horseback. One, two. . .three! Dustin and Jakob had found Isaac!

"Praise the Lord!" She snatched up her skirts and hurried to meet them. After six days, they'd come home. "Isaac!" Her little brother rode between Jakob on the left, and. . .Rawhide. The third man wasn't Dustin.

"Where is my husband?" she blurted out as soon as the trio reached her. She was vaguely aware of Mama, Gilda, and Kaitlin bustling up beside her.

"We split up to cover more ground." Jakob swung out of the

saddle. "He headed due east."

Still disappointed that Dustin hadn't returned with them, the knowledge that no tragedy had befallen him allowed her to breathe again.

"Mein Isaac!" Mama all but smothered him in a tight embrace before stepping back and giving him a rough shake, berating him in a flood of German before she hugged him once more. "Never do this again."

"I won't." Isaac squirmed from her grasp and stared at the toes of his boots.

"We're glad to have you home." Delana spoke past a lump in her throat.

When the horses were lodged in the barn, Mama herded everyone into the cabin she shared with Jakob and Isaac.

She had the men sitting at her table in no time, each with a cup of milk and some ginger drop cookies.

"Where did you find him?" Mama sat between Isaac and Jakob. "Fort Benton?"

"Rawhide found him." Jakob shook his head. "They told me he'd bought passage on a steamboat that had left forty minutes before I even arrived."

"You?" Mama stared at Rawhide. "You brought my son back to me?"

"Yep." Rawhide swallowed another cookie. "I was in town on business and was surprised to see Isaac there. When I found out what he was up to. . ." He shrugged.

"Rawhide talked some sense into me," Isaac finished. "Said it was a powerfully foolish plan. Told me my death wouldn't win the war—just make the rest of my family grieve." He looked down at his cup. "I didn't want to put you through that sadness again. I just felt like I had to do something so Hans's death mattered."

"So I told him that instead of shedding blood, the best thing he could do to honor his brother's memory was prove him right." Rawhide wiped his mouth with the back of his hand, but Mama just pushed another plate of cookies toward him.

"Rawhide says men like us, who make our own way and live by the work of their hands, show that America doesn't need slaves to be successful. Hans fought so that all people can have the right to build their own lives.

"I aim to help us prove up and make the farm a success and show that Hans was right—real men don't live off the work of others."

Tears of joy slipped silently down Delana's cheeks as she listened to her little brother. He wasn't so little anymore. Rawhide had done what she and Mama couldn't—talk to Isaac man-to-man. He'd been making his own way far longer than Jakob, and with the weight of experience behind his words, Rawhide had gotten through to Isaac. She couldn't begin to express her gratitude.

"Rawhide." Mama broke ties with propriety and reached across the table to take both his hands in hers. "Thank you for taking my baby boy and giving him back to me a man. I can never repay so much joy."

"Well, Bernadine. . ." Rawhide stared at their intertwined hands before gazing into her eyes. A slow smile spread across his face as he suggested, "You could always marry me."

eighteen

With a heavy heart and an empty stomach, Dustin returned home. Not even the sight of the three cozy cabins could distill the weight of his failure. He stabled his horse before heading toward his house with the benefit of light from a barn lantern.

He knocked at his own door, dreading what would come next. Delana peeked around the blue gingham curtains, and her eyes widened with happiness as she caught sight of him. Dustin hated the thought that her joy at seeing him would dwindle away when she heard he had not found her brother.

"Dustin!" She swung open the door and flung herself into his arms. Warmth seeped from the cabin into the unexpectedly cold night as he held her close.

He followed her inside but didn't sit down as she busied herself at the stove.

"You must be famished. Let me warm a few biscuits and whip up some gravy."

"Wait." The pressure of his hand on her arm turned her to face him. "Isaac is not with Jakob and your mother." He broke the bad news as gently as he could.

"Did he decide to sleep in the barn with Rawhide?" Delana's lack of concern made his chest ache.

Her faith in me is so strong that she can't imagine I didn't find her brother. She thinks she's fixing supper for her triumphant husband, but I have to tell her the truth.

"Delana, I didn't meet Rawhide or find Isaac at all." He waited for her shoulders to slump.

"Then they weren't in the barn?" She shrugged as though the motion would carry away the bad news.

"No. I don't know where either of them is, Delana." He searched her face for any hint of understanding.

"Neither do I, but I'm sure they'll turn up." She patted his shoulder and smiled brightly. "I'm so glad we don't have to worry anymore!"

Dustin pinched the bridge of his nose, drew a deep breath, and tried again. "I didn't bring Isaac home."

"How could you?" Delana's brow crinkled in puzzlement. "Rawhide found him at Fort Benton and talked sense into him."

"He's home?" Dustin asked incredulously.

"For two days now. Jakob was so relieved to find the pair of them. . . Now that you're here, everyone is happy again." She put her arms around him and pressed her cheek to his chest.

"Everyone's happy." Dustin closed his arms around her, relief overflowing his thoughts.

"Well, almost." Delana leaned back and tucked a shock of his hair behind his ear. "Rawhide asked Mama to marry him, and she hasn't said yes yet."

"Rawhide and *your mother*?" Dustin thought of the unlikely pair and shook his head.

"Not yet." Delana drew away to warm some biscuits in the oven. "But I think she'll say yes eventually."

Dustin sat down to mull this over. He drew off his pack and remembered the kitten. "I did bring a little something back for you."

"Oh?" She blinked. "What did you find in the middle of the wilderness?"

"Just a little *Paket*." Dustin named the kitten the German word for package, hoping to heighten Delana's curiosity.

"A package on the plains?"

"Of sorts." Dustin lifted the flap on his saddlebag, and the kitten thrust his head out to mew sleepily.

"A kitten!" Delana scooped the fur ball into her arms, looking at her present in astonishment.

"He crawled into my pack one night." Dustin grinned as Delana rubbed her cheek against Paket's soft fur.

"However did he wind up out there?" She wiggled her index finger, and the kitten playfully batted at it. "He's so small!"

"Perhaps a family headed for Virginia City lost him, though I'm not really sure. He's old enough to have been weaned." Dustin stood alongside her and ran a finger down the kitten's nose. "I thought he'd make a good addition to our home."

"I love him." Delana raised on tiptoe to give him a peck on the cheek before handing Paket to him.

"It's a relief to know everything's back to normal." Dustin took a huge bite of the biscuits and gravy she set before him.

"Not entirely," Delana hedged.

"Oh." Dustin swallowed. "Except for Rawhide and your mother." He still couldn't wrap his mind around the idea of those two as a couple. "We're one big, happy family." He fed Paket a bit of biscuit.

"Yes, we are." Delana took his left hand in hers and sat beside him. "And we're about to get bigger." She placed his hand on her abdomen.

"A babe?" His mouth suddenly dry, Dustin gulped down

some water. "You're expecting a child?"

"Yes." Delana nodded happily. "*We're* expecting our first child."

"When did you. . . when will it. . ." Dustin took a deep breath.

"I believe we conceived on our wedding night," Delana answered his half-spoken question.

That was in May. Dustin did some rapid counting. *June, July—she's two months along. August, September, October, November, December, January, February. . . Oh, no!*

"You'll give birth in February." He closed his eyes at the prospect.

"Soon after Christmas," Delana affirmed. "Isn't it wonderful timing?"

"No!" The crestfallen look on her face made him soften his response. "We'll be snowed in, Delana. There are no doctors, no midwives. . .no help at all."

"We'll be just fine." She put her hand to her stomach and gave a soft smile. "Women have been having babies since long before doctors."

And dying from childbirth for just as long. Dustin thought of his own mother. Neither she nor his younger sister had survived the ordeal.

"You won't." He made the decision. "Come September, I'll take you and your mother to Fort Benton. You'll get the help you need, and I'll come back for you after the spring thaw."

"What?" Disbelief was written on every line of her face. "You'd send me away?"

"There is no other choice."

"Yes, there is." She wrapped her arms around herself. "You could love me and stay beside me as I bring our child into the world."

"Not possible." He dismissed the notion. "Unless I leave with you in September, I'll be snowed in. If I go with you, I'll be stuck at Fort Benton until the thaw in March or even April. That's seven months or perhaps up to eight."

"Yet that's what you'd have me do." Delana's lower lip began to tremble.

"That's different." He had to make her understand. "If I leave for seven months, I forfeit our claim. One of the conditions of proving up is that I stay here over six months out of a year."

"It's months from two different calendar years," she insisted.

"But we made our claim the April before this last. Our second of the five years runs from until April third again." Dustin stood up. "I can't go with you."

"I won't go without you." Delana made a wide gesture with one arm. "I don't want to leave our home at all!"

"You must—for your sake and the babe's."

"I'm not ill or frail." Delana planted her hands on her hips. "There's no reason to think there will be complications."

"And there's no reason to assume there won't be!" He belatedly realized he'd gotten louder and modified his tone. "There's no sense in denying the possibility."

"Just as there's no purpose in allowing fear to rob us of this joy." Delana glowered fiercely. "Our child was conceived in this house and will be raised in it. It's only natural that the birth take place here, as well."

"Not in the dead of winter." Dustin's jaw clenched as his wife refused to see reason. "As the head of this house, I've made the decision. You will go to Fort Benton in September, and I'll hear no more of it tonight."

❧

The next morning, Delana crawled out of bed without having slept. She pressed a cool, damp towel to her aching head before dressing. Moving quietly so as not to wake Dustin, she set about making breakfast. She looked at the array of food and couldn't imagine eating anything. Delana hadn't suffered morning sickness for a fortnight but knew she'd be able to keep nothing down this morning.

He'll change his mind. He has to change his mind.

She set about making breakfast, ignoring the familiar sounds of Dustin waking up until he stood beside her.

"What's for breakfast?"

"Gruel." She handed him a bowl. *If he wants to act like a little child, he'll eat like one.* The idea held a sort of poetic justice.

He downed his breakfast without another word passing between them, then stomped to the barn.

Delana looked at the thin, yet lumpy mixture and made a moue of disgust. He'd eaten it without a word of complaint.

I'm the one who's guilty of being childish. Shame flooded her. *I'm a married woman, soon to be a mother, and yet I allowed myself to be petty. But I don't want to leave my friends and family and be all alone during my first Christmas as a married woman. He'd have me tucked away at Fort Benton when I should be helping gather the harvest and putting up the fruits of our garden.*

Rosalind's first birthday will pass without me seeing her first steps or hearing her first words. What if Rawhide convinces Mama to marry him in the late fall, and I'm not here to wish her wedding blessings? Her heart cried out at the very thought.

"No," she told Paket, firmly stating the syllable and sitting down. "I won't go." Delana slipped to her knees. "I can't."

"Lord," she whispered, rocking gently back and forth, "I cannot leave my husband and home to bear a child in a strange place. The truth remains that I cannot change Dustin's mind about it either. Wives are to submit to their husbands, I know. But what if our husbands are making the wrong decisions?"

She thought of the time not long ago when she wanted nothing more than to have Dustin make the difficult decisions. "After Papa died, the thought of getting here, of being with Dustin, saw me through. I felt that if we were together, it would all somehow work out. Dustin would be strong for me, and things wouldn't be so hard."

Though she'd wept silently through the night, it seemed she had still more to cry as tears welled in her eyes. "We're here together now, but it's still so hard, Lord. I never questioned my faith in Dustin, my belief that he would do right by me and my family. Now I realize that I can't rely on my husband to spare me from all the pains in this world. I should never have put him on that pedestal in the first place. Dustin's strengths are to complement my own, not carry my burden.

"I ran to a man when I should have run to You. Yours is the strength beyond all measure to support us when we stumble. Yours is the love whose perfection forgives our frailties and carries our burdens." Peace flooded her as she acknowledged the truth.

"I put my faith in You, where it belongs, and trust that You will guide Dustin to see that he can't ease his fears by sending me to Fort Benton. Only trust in You can do that."

Delana rose to her feet, dried her tears, and went to ask her husband to pray about his decision.

nineteen

"What's this I hear about you proposing to Mama Albright?" Dustin found Rawhide in the barn.

"Depends on what the person said when he was talkin' to you." Rawhide leaned against the wall while Dustin mucked.

"Delana mentioned that you asked her mama to marry you." Dustin halted and leaned on his shovel.

"That's about the long and short of it." Rawhide scratched his beard.

"What made you do a thing like that? You've always been the most independent man I ever knew."

"Independence has its rewards, but a man can only stand his own company for so long." Rawhide grabbed a shovel. "Me being such an interesting fellow, I just managed to hold out longer than most."

"Why Mama Albright?" Dustin couldn't think of a tactful way to pose the question. "You two seem an unlikely couple."

"Why not Bernadine?" Rawhide stopped shoveling to glower at Dustin. "She misses her husband; I've gone through missing my first wife. We've got plenty in common. Both of us understand the value of day-to-day companionship."

Dustin winced as he thought of the long months when Delana would be at Fort Benton. Rawhide had a point about the companionship.

"I'm no expert," Dustin hedged. *Now there's an understatement.*

148

I can't even get my wife to a doctor when she's going to have a baby! "But it sounds to me as though you're talking from the head. Are you just being practical?"

"A man doesn't take on a woman like Bernadine Albright to be practical." Rawhide's statement defied contradiction. "I sure didn't choose her for the sake of convenience."

"Then why did you spout off all that about commonalities and companionship?" Dustin raised a brow. "What's the core of it?"

"Ah." Rawhide drew a deep breath. "There comes a time in a man's life when surprises are few and far between. Challenges that used to bring achievement seem hollow with no one to share them with. Now, Bernadine"—the older man chuckled as he spoke—"she's a surprising challenge."

"You wouldn't be looking for a merry chase, only to lose interest when you've caught your prize?" Dustin folded his arms across his chest. If he thought for even one instant that Rawhide was toying with his mother-in-law, the old wanderer would have a few acres less to roam around in.

"Nah, Bernadine's special. Sure, when I first met her I thought she was an uppity, too-starched kind of woman, but she's proven me wrong. The woman lost her son, husband, and home in a few short weeks. Instead of wailin' over it, she's pitched in around here." Rawhide took on a kind of goofy grin. "She's got a sparkle in her eye, brains in her head, and spirit in her soul. Life will never be dull if I can convince her she has room in her heart."

"In that case you might think of asking Jakob's blessing before you ask her again."

"What kind of a rascal do you think I am?" Rawhide seemed

affronted. "I got that before I tried it the first time!"

"How will you set about convincing her to say yes?" Dustin wondered if he could borrow any tactics to appease Delana.

"I figure I've got a mighty fine start, seein' as how I led her out here, helped build the cabins, and brought her son back to her in one piece." Rawhide leaned the shovel against a wall. "Then there's the fact that, with the freight drivers gone for over two months, I'm the only eligible man for her in these parts. Those are good odds."

"Can't hurt." Dustin didn't bother to hide his grin. "Assuming she wants to remarry."

"Now don't go throwing a wrench in the works." Rawhide shook a finger at him. "I'll pay her court: say nice things, pick her some flowers, weed her garden, and anything else I can think of."

"I can think of something that couldn't hurt." Dustin's eyes narrowed speculatively. "You could escort her and Delana to Fort Benton this winter and see that her daughter delivers her grandchild safely."

&a

"Delana!" Kaitlin came rushing toward her.

"What is it?" Delana stopped and waited for her friend to catch up.

"I dinna want to bear tales," her friend worried, "but I overheard Dustin say something I know would upset you. You should be forewarned."

"Did he mention his plan to send me to Fort Benton for the winter, by any chance?" Delana patted Kaitlin's arm. "I already know. Why don't you come for a walk with me? We might find a patch of wild mint for a pitcher of tea."

"Mam's with Rosalind, so I dinna see why not." Kaitlin fell into step beside her. "I'm surprised to see you so tranquil. When last he spoke of sending you away, it seemed so devastating. Aren't you going to fight this decision?"

"I already have." Delana sucked in a breath at the recollection. "When I shared my joyous news, he immediately calculated that the baby will come sometime in February. Instead of sharing my elation that we'd have another wonderful event after Christmas, he spoke of our isolation and the harsh winter."

"Oh, that's a pity." Kaitlin shook her head. "Did he say naught of his pleasure at being made a father?"

"Not a word." Delana twisted her handkerchief. "His thoughts were for doctors and midwives. That's when he concocted this outlandish scheme to send me to the fort."

"This canna be allowed. When is he fixin' to send you?" Kaitlin huffed. "We'll need time to change his mind."

"I already told him I didn't want to leave. Reminders of my good health did not sway him, nor the prospect of a seven- or eight-month separation. He doesn't heed my wishes."

"Oooh." Kaitlin's eyes scrunched in anger. "How can you not be affected by the way he ignores your words?"

"Believe me"—Delana grimaced ruefully—"I was affected. Enough so that I made him lumpy gruel for breakfast. He ate it without a word of complaint. When he left for the barn, I dissolved into tears. Only then did I do what I should have long before—pray."

"So you've the peace of the Lord about you," Kaitlin surmised. "That explains it."

"Confiding in God all my hurt and disappointment made

me realize I hadn't turned to Him as my rock since Papa's death. Dustin has agreed to pray on the matter, so I need to trust that the Lord will soften Dustin's heart on this issue." Delana grinned. "Failing that, surely the Almighty can work on his hard head!"

"I dinna envy that task." Kaitlin giggled. "Arthur can be the same way when he gets ahold of some strange notion."

"It must have something to do with being male," Delana mused. "Rawhide may not have proposed to Mama again, but he hasn't backed down, either."

"Since when is loving your mother a strange notion?" Kaitlin gave her a soft nudge.

"That's not the part I take issue with." Delana headed toward a small hill filled with lush plants. "The way he just slipped his proposal into the conversation was all but guaranteed not to sit well with Mama."

" 'Twas sudden." Kaitlin thought a moment. "Do you think she would have him if he wooed her properly?"

"I hope so." Delana thought of the times Rawhide had coaxed a sparkle into her mother's eyes. "And I think we'll find out soon enough. Yesterday he asked me what her favorite wildflower is."

"That's better." Kaitlin stopped and sniffed the air. "The scent of mint freshens the breeze." She turned toward the soft wind and walked west.

"Here it is!" Delana bent to pick a few sprigs. The invigorating scent grew stronger as she gathered. "I've had a craving for mint of late and plucked my first patch bare." She placed one of the silver-green leaves on her tongue, letting the flavor refresh her.

"You should plant some in the garden so it's right at hand." Kaitlin carefully dug up one of the plants, roots and all.

"Summer is late to be planting anything," Delana said, "though it can't hurt to try. I'll be making a large batch of tea with these. It will be ready tomorrow."

"We should gather more while it's plentiful and dry some." Kaitlin filled her own apron pockets. " 'Tis good for the stomach, they say."

"I've heard that before, though I don't know much about herbs." Delana straightened. "It's something I would like to learn about."

"Mam knows a bit. She'll tell you to take a tea made of red raspberry leaf every day for the last month or so until you come to term." Kaitlin fell into step with Delana. "I took it when I was close to birthing my Rosalind."

"What does it do?"

" 'Tis good for the womb and eases the way for childbearing." Kaitlin smiled. "Scotswomen have used it for hundreds of years."

"I'll be sure to remember that." Delana stepped around a fallen tree. "It's fortunate that raspberries grow here!"

" 'Tis wonderful how the Lord provides."

"Yes." Delana put a hand over her stomach, thinking of the child within. "We are blessed."

ࢲ

"Nein." Dustin widened his stance, refusing to let her pass. "Women who are expecting children do not ride horses."

"Then let's look on it as a marvelous surprise not to be expected, but anticipated." When Delana tried to sidle around him, he picked her up by the waist and set her outside the barn once again.

"It's too high," he protested. *She has to know it's not safe. What if she falls?*

"I'll choose a short horse," she promised. "It's not as though I'm planning on climbing a tree."

He crossed his arms over his chest. "Don't get any ideas."

"I'm only in my fourth month, darling." Delana laid a hand on his arm. "Staying active is the best thing I can do for me and our child."

"Uh-uh." Dustin shook his head. "If you feel the need to move around, go for a walk. Just not in the forest." He suddenly thought of Kaitlin's wrenched ankle. "And not alone."

"Anything else?" His wife scowled at him, and Dustin bit back a smile. She was about as intimidating as a fluffy chick.

"Don't wander too far," he added, just for good measure.

"Would you like to hammer a post into the ground, attach a short rope to it, and tie the other end about my waist?" She jabbed him in the chest. "I'm not a child. I'm just carrying one!"

"Exactly." He turned the words around on her. "Everywhere you go, so does our baby. Would you let a baby get up on a horse? Or climb a tree? Or wander about in the forest alone?"

"It's not the same, and you know it." She gritted her teeth. "And don't act as though you're being reasonable. You won't let me climb the ladder to the loft or stand on one of the benches to reach the top shelf."

"Those are both reasonable." He mentally patted himself on the back for his vigilance.

"You won't let me build a stool—the bench is the only thing I can use." Obviously exasperated, she bunched the fabric of his shirt in her hand.

"Now, be fair." Dustin winced as she caught some chest hair in that grip. "I wouldn't let you build a stool even if you weren't pregnant."

"You're impossible!" She let him go and turned to stalk away, the little gray cat trailing behind her.

"I love you, too," he called after her, rubbing the sore spot on his chest. *How can she accuse me of being unreasonable?*

twenty

"BERNADINE ALBRIGHT," Rawhide rode along the western edge of their property, bellowing with all his might. "I'M FIXIN' ON HAVING YOU TO BE MY BRIDE, SO I'M ANNOUNCING MY INTENTIONS TO ONE AND ALL."

Of the entire Montana Territory, Delana mentally tacked on. She watched as Mama released the handles of the wheelbarrow, a dull *thunk* sounding as it hit the ground. She saw her mother's eyes widen in shock before narrowing in anger.

"Foolish man!" Mama's full skirts made her look as though she sailed on the grasses of the plains as Rawhide kept on hollering at the top of his lungs.

"I'VE PURCHASED THE LAND ALONG YOUR WESTERN BORDER, FREE AND CLEAR. YOU'LL SEE THAT I AIM TO SETTLE DOWN WHERE WE CAN BE CLOSE TO YOUR CHILDREN."

He has to see her coming. Delana knew that Mama in a temper was practically impossible to ignore. *He'll stop shouting at any moment. There, he's stopped now. . .* Her thoughts slowed as her step quickened. *He just drew breath to keep right on bellowing. If the man has a lick of sense, he'd—*

"Rawhide Jones," Mama commanded, "turn that horse and ride off until you're fit for polite company."

"NO!" Rawhide's shout made everyone wince, and he cleared his throat. "Not possible, Bernadine."

"You've made a fool of yourself, riding this border and shouting like a man who's taken leave of his senses." Mama shook her index finger at him. "And after I already told you I'd not remarry with my husband not even a year gone. The very idea!" She huffed. "Scandalous."

"So long as I have your attention." Rawhide leaned forward and, instead of riding his horse away as quickly as it could carry him, swung out of the saddle to stand toe-to-toe with Delana's outraged mother. "Mark my words, Bernadine Albright, I'll wait for you to grieve your first husband. I'll wait for you to see past my rough manners. Whenever you decide you want me, know that I'll be here."

"It will be a long wait." Bernadine shook her head. "I loved my Otto." Tears thickened her words. "He cannot be replaced."

Delana fought between the urge to comfort her mama and the obvious need for the two stubborn souls to reach some kind of understanding.

"I respect that." Rawhide's reply seemed solemnly sincere. "No one will ever be like my Fredericka. . .and that's as it should be."

"Ja," Mama whispered her agreement.

"But there are many things left here to share." Rawhide's gesture encompassed the mountains, forests, and meadows around them. "I'll wait if it means I can share these joys with you."

Mama didn't say another word.

"Of course," Rawhide began as he swung back into his saddle, "I figure I might have to pester you every so often—just so you know I'm still here. Besides"—he grinned—"a man can get mighty hungry during a long wait."

Waiting can be so difficult. Delana sighed. The heat of the sun beating down upon her did little to warm her heart.

The first of September seemed every bit as hot as the summer months before. Even so, Delana feared change in the wind. She and Dustin hadn't spoken about Fort Benton since the night she'd told him he was to become a father.

Lord, he promised to pray about it and listen for Your answer. I've waited on You and trusted that whatever decision Dustin came to, it would be the right one for our family. Now it's coming to the time when I need to know what to prepare myself for. If it is Your will that I leave, then it must be for the safety of our child and I will go. I cannot pretend to understand Your ways. . .but I need time to be able to say good-bye to my husband and home, friends and family.

Mama noticed her preoccupation, but Delana couldn't explain it. This was something between a husband and wife. What mama thought bore no consequence; the matter belonged in the Lord's hands.

Since the only thing Mama thought could be distracting her daughter was the baby, she took to telling birth stories at random moments. This morning Kaitlin happened to mention an unfortunate yearning for pickles.

"I remember my sister Hildegarde going into labor. She demanded pickles during the early hours. Her husband got them for her, and she ate so many we couldn't see how they fit. Later, she upset her stomach." Mama grimaced. "She would never eat another pickle."

Delana grimaced. Some stories just shouldn't be told. For

all her attempts to be encouraging, Mama made her even more uncomfortable.

The only person whom she could talk to about her uncertainty was Kaitlin.

"Surely Dustin would have told me if he changed his mind? He'd let me know." Delana drummed her fingers on the side of the bench. "Last he told me, I'm going."

"Maybe since he hasn't set you to packing, he assumes you know you're not." Kaitlin frowned. "That didn't come out right, but I meant to say that he would have you preparing for the journey if you were still to leave."

"Unless he hasn't made the final decision." Delana stood and paced around her kitchen. "I know I said I'd trust the Lord's will. . .but I had thought to know what it was!"

"You're a stronger woman than I." Kaitlin's eyes grew sad. "I missed my Arthur so much while I carried Rosalind. I missed his strength. I wished I coulda held his hand. . ." She shook her head. "Carrying a babe is a wondrously frightening time. Your husband should be with you to help."

"He hovers too much as is," Delana grumbled. "I can hardly step foot outside the door!"

"I ken he frustrates you with his fussin'." Kaitlin smiled wistfully. "All the same, I see it as a measure of his love. No man hovers unless it's love."

"I think you're right, but for now it's exasperating. I've no way of knowing if he'll send me away or keep shadowing my every move."

"Well. . .you could pack a few things," Kaitlin said. "To prepare yourself if he persists with his cockamamie plan."

"Now that's an idea." Delana considered it. "If I pack, it

shows Dustin that I trust the decision he made so many weeks ago. On the other hand, if he's changed his mind, he'll tell me so! Either way, at least I'll know what we'll be dealing with."

With her plan made, Delana resolved not to waste any time putting it into motion.

৯

September has arrived, Lord. I know that I have to send my wife away, but I can't imagine spending so many months without Delana. Her safety and that of our child come before lesser desires. The time when I must say good-bye draws close, and I have yet to tell her.

I've prayed and waited to see whether I would experience a change of heart. Even after all these weeks, I know my responsibilities haven't changed. Still, I dread telling her. She's been so patient, never pushing me to finalize my decision. I know Delana feels strongly that she belongs here, but I cannot in good conscience allow her to stay. Emotions don't take precedence over logic.

All the same, Lord, I'm asking for Your help in facing my wife.

twenty-one

"You look like a man with a lot on his mind." Arthur brushed bits of straw from his shirt as he stepped out of the barn.

"Tonight I need to tell Delana I'm sending her to Fort Benton through the winter." Dustin let loose a heavy sigh. "She's not going to like it."

"I see." Arthur leaned against the doorframe. "Kaitlin mentioned something like that might be on the wind."

"Oh?" Dustin frowned. "I never spoke with her about it." *I'd hate to think Delana was taking a matter to others that should remain between us and the Lord.*

"She overheard you make a comment to Rawhide several weeks ago and asked Delana about it." Arthur raised a thick black brow. "Would you take kindly to a few well-meant words from an old friend?"

"Depends on what those words are." Dustin bristled at the idea of being told how to handle his marriage.

"I'll tread carefully then. All I can share is my own experience—you take from it what you will."

"Fair enough." Dustin relaxed his rigid stance. Arthur wasn't one to use his words lightly.

"You'll recall that I wasna wi' my Kaitlin when she carried our wee Rosalind." Arthur waited for Dustin's nod before continuing. "I dinna know she expected our child when I left her in Baltimore."

"And if you had?" Dustin opened his canteen. "What would your decision have been? To leave her, to take her into an isolated wilderness, or to forfeit the future of your family altogether?"

"That I canna say, as I was never put in that position." Arthur folded his arms across his massive chest. "I dinna favor any of those choices, just as you see no perfect solution to your own dilemma."

"This much I've considered on my own." Dustin took a swig of his water. "I've thought on it often."

"I'd expect no less. But I'd count myself a poor friend to both you and Delana if I dinna tell you how deeply I regret missing that special time. My Kaitlin couldna lean on me when she dinna feel well. I canna go back and give her the comfort she needed when I was miles away."

Arthur's remorse sliced through Dustin. *Delana will go through the same thing if I send her to Fort Benton.* He shook his head. *What am I thinking? There is no if—it is the safest place for her and our child.*

"Since Kaitlin stayed in Baltimore, she had all the resources and help she'd need were she or the babe in danger." Dustin referenced his main reason for the decision he'd made. "Delana will have the same help to ensure she and our child are safe."

"That's a powerful reason to send her," Arthur admitted. "But the state of a woman's heart affects her health. What if she needs your love and support more than the science of a doctor?"

"There's no way to know that." Dustin dismissed the notion. "Besides, she carries my love wherever she goes."

"Did that knowledge stop you from missing Delana during the year you spent apart?"

No. I thought of her every day, wondering if all was well with her, if she would be happy here with me. But such musings do no good.

"The knowledge that I did what was best for our future eased the sacrifice."

"And if you werena certain that was best for your family's future—as Delana isna sure?" Arthur's quiet words tore into Dustin like sharp daggers.

"It will only be a short time."

"Seven months away from your wife isna significant?" The blacksmith shook his head. "We both know 'tis not true."

"What would you have me do?" Dustin clenched his fists. "Allow her to stay at the risk of her life and the life of our child?"

"Pray." Arthur walked up to him, placing one large hand on Dustin's shoulder. "I would have you pray."

"I have. My decision remains."

"Dustin, let me ask you something." Arthur stayed by his side until he assented. "When you prayed, did you ask for the Lord to reveal His will. . .or did you ask Him to support yours?"

With that, his friend left Dustin to his own thoughts.

There is nothing I will not do to protect my family—even unto being without my wife through the long winter. He began to walk toward home. *How dare Arthur question my obedience to God! I've asked Him time and again to help Delana realize what must be done.*

The thought stopped him in his tracks. *Lord, is it possible that I've prayed for You to do my will instead of me seeking Yours? Every time I've come to You it has been to ask for what is best for my family.*

"But I've asked for what *I* think is best." The realization staggered him even as he spoke it aloud.

Lord, I ask Your forgiveness for my shortsightedness. Please give me a sign. . .something to show me what You would have me do. I'll not say a word to Delana until I'm certain of Your will.

ક

Delana took her valise from her trunk that very night, determined to end the matter once and for all. *Whether the answer is what I hope for or not, it will be settled.*

Dustin gave her an astonished look as she plopped it on the bed and began adding hankies, a nightgown, and her cloak. Two dresses followed the other items. Paket, now almost double the size he'd been when he'd arrived, tried to wriggle into the valise. Delana fished him out and set him on the bed.

"What are you doing?" Dustin's deep rumble sounded behind her.

He's going to tell me I'm not going, that I shouldn't be packing! Delana calmly folded a blanket and placed it inside. "I'm packing." She held her breath and waited for him to tell her to unpack.

"All right." The weight of those two words made her shoulders stoop for a moment. "Since you've changed your mind. . ."

"I didn't change my mind." Delana turned to face him. "I'm trusting you. Though I must say, I thought you'd come to a different conclusion."

"How so? This is the best way to see that you and our child

are well cared for." Dustin drew her into a hug. "I pledged before God and man to protect you and care for you all the days of my life."

"I thought of other things," Delana admitted. "Yet I know you prayed over the matter and feel led to choose this path. I will follow you."

"I asked the Lord for a sign as to whether you should go or stay." Dustin tilted her chin. "Your trust in abiding by the decision you thought I'd already made ended the matter. The moment I saw you pack, I knew what we were to do."

"No!" Delana pulled away and shut the valise with a sharp snap. *My desperation for a decision can't push him toward the wrong one!*

"I couldn't know whether you didn't speak of it because you felt the matter already settled, or if your silence meant it was no longer an issue." She struggled to remain calm. "After so much time, I expected to have you tell me clearly once and for all."

"So you're not ready to go to Fort Benton, although it is the safest decision for you and our child." Dustin sank down onto the edge of the bed. "Why can nothing be simple?"

"I was ready to honor the path the Lord revealed to you." Delana sat beside him and reached to take his hand in hers. "That changes if you don't have a peace about this decision."

"What I don't have peace about is upsetting you." Dustin rubbed his temples. "You will be protected to the best of my ability—what more is there to consider?"

"Do you want me to tell you what I think?" Delana spoke quietly, hoping her husband would choose to hear her. "Whether my thoughts sway your decision or not, I'll be satisfied to know that you considered them." *Lord, please let him say yes!*

"You are my wife." Dustin met her gaze squarely. "The hopes of your heart are things to be shared. Tell me."

&

Whatever concerns she has, I'll do my best to alleviate them before seeing her to Fort Benton. Delana honors me as the head of our home by accepting my decision; it is good that I should honor her views in return.

"I think of living without you for seven months." Her eyes shone with unshed tears. "How can I not share each day with you when our child grows within me?"

"It is a long time," he conceded. "Try to understand I think of sharing years with both of you once you are safely delivered of our son or daughter." He rubbed his thumb over the sensitive skin on the back of her hand. "I'm willing to trade a few months to safeguard our life together."

"I remember Psalm 128: 'Thy wife shall be as a fruitful vine by the sides of thine house.' Our family is multiplying as we are instructed, but you consider sending me away from our home."

"We'll raise our child here, along with any brothers and sisters the Lord sees fit to give us." His reassurances seemed to have little effect.

"The scriptures tell us that children are the heritage of the Lord, and the prophet Ezekiel exhorts a mother to be joyful with her children." Delana looked down at their joined hands. "That joy is halved when we're apart. How can my heart be full when my child takes me away from the man I love?"

Dustin sucked in a sharp breath. "I love you, and I'll miss you while you're gone. Remember, though, that I will come for both of you. We do this to ensure our family is whole."

"And if it is best for the child, is it best for our marriage?" Delana bit her lip before continuing. "A husband is told to cleave unto his wife, and also to live joyfully with her."

"I am joyful when I am with you." He smoothed her hair with his palm. "A few months won't take that away."

"And what of Matthew's warning about man and wife— that what God hath joined together, let no man put asunder?" She paused a moment. "Are we not dividing ourselves when it is unnecessary?"

"I believe it is necessary." He drew her into his arms, though she suddenly stiffened and went absolutely still. "Are you all right?" He fought to remain calm. *What if, in my determination to be sure she stays healthy, I push her toward illness?*

"The baby. . ." Delana's voice held wonder, not pain. "He just kicked."

"Where?" Dustin flattened his palm over her stomach, trying to feel the force of a tiny foot.

"Kaitlin and Mama are right. . .it's as though a butterfly just fluttered beneath my ribs." Delana took his hand in both of hers. "You won't be able to feel him, yet. Not until he's much bigger."

"I'm going to miss it." Gloom invaded the cabin as Dustin realized this was something he couldn't share with her.

"Oh," Delana gave a tiny gasp. "There he goes again." Her eyes shone with happiness. "I can feel him moving!"

"Him?" Dustin wondered if she even knew she'd said it.

"A son." She nodded. "Somehow, I just know our firstborn is a son."

"A son," Dustin repeated, humbled. "Our son."

"Yes."

"When will I be able to feel him?"

"It will be months still before the time comes." She cradled her abdomen lovingly. "All things in God's time."

All things in God's time. The words knocked the air from Dustin's chest. *God chose to give us this baby now—He timed it so our child would be born in winter. Just as he brought Delana to me a year in advance. I've tried to create a timetable, and God moves things along at His own pace. It's beyond my control.*

"You're not going to Fort Benton." Dustin cuddled her close. "God gave us the child now, and I have to trust His plan. It's just like my father's favorite verse."

"What verse is that?" Delana smiled up at him.

" 'To every thing there is a season, and a time to every purpose under the heaven.' Seasons change, time goes on, and God guides us away from our own plans. My father knew this, and he always claimed the third chapter in Ecclesiastes spoke to the farmer in him." Dustin stood, drawing his wife to her feet along with him.

" 'A time to plant. . .' " She looked at her tummy and smiled.

" 'And a time to pluck up that which is planted,' " Dustin finished. "We'll gather the sweet harvest together."

epilogue

April 1868

"We did it!" Dustin's words made Delana leap into his arms.

"You have the deed?" She tried to rummage through his pockets.

"Right here." He handed it to her. "One hundred and sixty acres, free and clear to Dustin Friemont."

"You worked so hard." Delana rested her hand on his arm. "I'm so proud."

"We worked hard. I couldn't have done it without you." He rubbed his thumb across the sensitive skin at the base of her neck, making Delana shiver.

"Five years and one hundred and twenty acres cultivated." She smiled up at her hardworking husband. "The Homestead Act meant we only needed to plant on forty."

"Our home is worth the effort." He looked over her shoulder. "Our family deserves it."

"Daddy!" Bart raced up to his parents, his little brother's shorter legs churning at a furious pace to keep up. "You're back!"

"I sure am." Dustin stooped to embrace their sons.

"Good to see you!" Arthur clapped him on the back as he stood up.

"From the smile on your face, I see you've officially proven up." Jakob and Isaac joined the group.

"It is wunderbar." Mama beamed at them.

"This deserves a celebration!" Gilda and Kaitlin each held two fresh raspberry pies.

"Good news always does." Rawhide looked at Mama. "But good news can always be added to."

"Rawhide," Mama spoke so softly Delana almost couldn't hear her.

"Bernadine." He stepped closer, clasping both her hands in his. "Your worth is beyond rubies—certainly deserving of a man's patience. I waited as you grieved for your first husband. Then I waited as you devoted yourself to your handsome grandbabies. I've held out for the three and a half years since you first turned me down, knowing your need to help your children establish themselves. Now they have. It is time to think about your own happiness—and mine." He sank down on one knee before her, never releasing her hands. "Bernadine Albright, will you marry me?"

"Oh, Rawhide." Mama's eyes sparkled with unshed tears. "It's about time you asked me again."

A Letter To Our Readers

Dear Reader:

In order that we might better contribute to your reading enjoyment, we would appreciate your taking a few minutes to respond to the following questions. We welcome your comments and read each form and letter we receive. When completed, please return to the following:

Fiction Editor
Heartsong Presents
PO Box 719
Uhrichsville, Ohio 44683

1. Did you enjoy reading *A Time to Plant* by Kelly Eileen Hake?
   ❏ Very much! I would like to see more books by this author!
   ❏ Moderately. I would have enjoyed it more if

   _____

   _____

   _____

2. Are you a member of **Heartsong Presents**?   ❏ Yes   ❏ No
   If no, where did you purchase this book? _____

   _____

3. How would you rate, on a scale from 1 (poor) to 5 (superior), the cover design? _____

4. On a scale from 1 (poor) to 10 (superior), please rate the following elements.

   ____ Heroine   ____ Plot
   ____ Hero   ____ Inspirational theme
   ____ Setting   ____ Secondary characters

5. These characters were special because? _____

_____

_____

6. How has this book inspired your life? _____

_____

_____

7. What settings would you like to see covered in future
   Heartsong Presents books? _____

_____

_____

8. What are some inspirational themes you would like to see
   treated in future books? _____

_____

_____

9. Would you be interested in reading other **Heartsong
   Presents** titles? ❏ Yes   ❏ No

10. Please check your age range:

    ❏ Under 18   ❏ 18-24
    ❏ 25-34   ❏ 35-45
    ❏ 46-55   ❏ Over 55

Name _____

Occupation _____

Address _____

City, State, Zip_____

TEXAS
BRIDES

3 stories in 1

Travel along with three Scottish men as they make Texas their home. Discover the joys and sorrows of starting life anew and testing the waters of innocent love.

Titles by author Cathy Marie Hake include: *To Love Mercy*, *To Walk Humbly*, and *To Do Justice*.

Historical, paperback, 352 pages, 5³/₁₆" x 8"

Heart♥ong

Presents